As kisses went, this one rated well beyond Monica's high standards.

She struggled to figure out exactly where in the stratosphere it compared, then gave up and simply sank in.

Wrapping her arms around his neck, pulling him closer, made it more a pleasure in the present than one just swirling around in her mind. Beneath her arms she felt the strength of his broad shoulders. Pressing against her with heated persistence, the delicious warmth of an aroused man. Her heart hammered as his tongue slipped fiercely into her mouth. He was consuming her, that's what she thought when coherent words surfaced. He was sucking and tasting, savoring and enticing. She was simply falling, falling, until she didn't think she could feel the floor beneath her feet.

Then, as quickly as this pleasurable funnel cloud had swooped her up, it dropped her. Hot to cold, light to dark, beginning to end. Alex pulled back, stared down at her, then walked away.

Again.

Books by A.C. Arthur

Kimani Romance

Love Me Like No Other
A Cinderella Affair
Guarding His Body
Second Chance, Baby
Defying Desire
Full House Seduction
Summer Heat
Sing Your Pleasure
Touch of Fate
Winter Kisses

ARTIST C. ARTHUR

was born and raised in Baltimore, Maryland, where she currently resides with her husband and three children. An active imagination and a love for reading encouraged her to begin writing in high school and she hasn't stopped since.

Determined to bring a new edge to romance, she continues to develop intriguing plots, racy characters and fresh dialogue—thus keeping readers on their toes!

Visit her website, www.acarthur.net.

Winter KISSES

A.C. ARTHUR

KIMANI
ROMANCE

To anyone who has ever struggled with a secret,
a past that you felt no one would ever understand.
Here's to forgiveness and brighter days.

KIMANI PRESS™

Recycling programs
for this product may
not exist in your area.

ISBN-13: 978-0-373-86237-5

WINTER KISSES

Copyright © 2011 by Artist C. Arthur

www.kimanipress.com

Printed in U.S.A.

Dear Reader,

It's finally Monica's turn! When I started the stories of the Lakefield sisters I knew Monica would be last because she had the most baggage and the longest road to true love. I didn't really know which man would be the one to tame her, but after *Summer Heat* I was sure that Alex Bennett was the one.

This story may touch a few hearts, bring a few laughs or even grunts of disapproval, but it's so truly Monica's story, her voyage through uncharted waters. Sometimes it's hard for a strong, independent woman to sit still and listen, really listen to her heart. I'm glad Monica did just that and I'm very happy that Alex was the one talking to her.

So as *Winter Kisses* concludes the Lakefield sisters, it opens the door for the Donovan cousins to take the lead. After this wintry love affair, get prepared for the heat of Miami Beach and the lives and loves of Sean and Dion Donovan, coming next year!

As always, happy reading.

AC

Prologue

The Setup

"She's never going to go for this." Sam Desdune sipped from his glass of wine, looking over the rim at his wife.

Karena Lakefield-Desdune smiled. Marriage and living in the stress-free country house away from the city suited her just perfectly. "The most important thing to Monica is making sure Lakefield Galleries has a stellar reputation and continues to make money. If she thinks for one minute that my missing a meeting might jeopardize that, she'll go to the ends of the earth to fix the problem."

"And then she's going to come down on you so hard you'll wish you worked in another country," Sam added with a frown. "I don't want you taking on that kind of stress."

"I'll be fine, Sam. I'm pregnant, not fragile. I can deal with Monica's backlash."

"If your guy does his thing we won't have to worry about her backlash," Deena Lakefield-Donovan said from her perch on a stool at the bar. Standing right beside her with his hand wrapped securely around her shoulders was her husband of about six months, Maxwell Donovan.

"Matchmaking can be a dangerous game," Max added.

"And matchmaking with my brother is the most dangerous game of all." Renny Bennett sat on the leather couch with his wife, Sam's twin sister, Bree, beside him.

"I think it's time Alex settled down. He works way too hard and spends too much time trying to take care of his family. He needs to find someone special," Bree said.

"The operative word being 'find,' hence he needs to look for himself, not be conned into a meeting with a woman like Monica," Sam said.

"And just what's a woman like Monica?" Karena asked, trying not to sound offended.

Sam immediately lifted his hands in surrender while around his den the men looked away, hiding their chuckles. "Whoa, wait a minute. You know I love my sister-in-law. Monica and I have developed an amicable relationship in the time I've known her. But, baby, you know she's not an easy woman. I mean, if she was we wouldn't be sitting here plotting a way to get her laid."

"We are not plotting to get her laid!" Karena stated adamantly.

"We're not?" Deena gave Karena a perplexed look before putting her glass on the bar.

Bree laughed. "We're plotting to get both of them laid before they drive us all crazy."

"Fine, we can get Alex there without a problem. The rest is going to be up to them. If you ladies think they're such a good match then a cozy cabin on the slopes of Aspen couldn't be a better place for them to hook up. Now you just need to do your part." This was from Renny, who wasn't totally convinced but had learned long ago to pick and choose his arguments with his wife. She'd met Monica Lakefield while working with Sam's private investigation agency so she knew the woman and she knew Alex. He would have to trust her judgment, for now.

"Then it's settled. Karena, make the call," Deena said.

All eyes were on her as Karena picked up the cordless phone and began to dial.

"Monica?" she said a few seconds later. "We've got a problem."

Chapter 1

"Crap!" Monica blurted then looked around to make sure no one heard her. Kneeling quickly, she tried to rescue her BlackBerry that had fallen into a sloppy, wet slope of snow right near the steps.

Droplets of water spotted her white leather gloves as she reached into the snow and scooped up the phone. Her teeth clenched and she so badly wanted to curse again as she tried to shake the water from the phone. The screen was black. She pushed the menu button. Nothing. She pressed the on button. Nothing.

She took the wooden steps without even looking up and continued to study her phone, praying it would turn on. It didn't and then she was at the door so she slipped it into her pocket and walked inside. Her cheeks tingled as the frigidly cold air of Aspen, Colorado, which had just about frozen them, gave way to the welcome warmth of two huge fireplaces.

It was two days after Christmas, a Monday afternoon she should have been spending in her office going over the sales slips from last week's showing. Instead, she was walking up to the large marble-and-cherrywood counter with the gold sign reading Concierge. She wasn't at the gallery in Manhattan—instead, she was here at this ski resort to meet with two of Lakefield Galleries' biggest sponsors in the hopes of keeping their support for the Black History showing coming in a few short weeks.

The thought of Karena dropping the ball with the Mendlesons had Monica clenching her teeth again. At this rate she would be paying her orthodontist half her yearly salary. But lately her sisters and their carefree attitude and lifestyle were really starting to get on her nerves. Both her younger sisters were now what they called "happily married." She'd more aptly call it "blissfully stupid." Why they thought settling down with a man completed their lives in some way she had no clue. And she much preferred her own stance of "no marriage, no hassles."

"Reservation for Monica Lakefield," she said to the clerk whose name tag read Jack.

Jack happily tapped keys on the keyboard then looked up at her and smiled. "Ms. Lakefield, yes. You're in the western cabin, which is out this door and to your right, last cabin on the left. I'll have your bags brought down."

"Thank you. Let me get my credit card," she said, reaching into her purse to get her wallet.

Jack shook his head. "That won't be necessary. The bill has already been taken care of."

"Fine. Thank you," she said and dropped her wallet back into her bag.

Karena must have used the company card to make her reservation. That made sense, but she really didn't expect her sister to be using the brain she was blessed with. Especially because when Monica last talked to her at the airport, Karena was still at home with her husband. Neither of her sisters thought working on the weekend or the days after a holiday was a good idea. To the contrary, Monica lived by seven-day workweeks.

As she trudged through the ice-slicked walkway, she thought maybe she should have put on sturdier boots. As it was, her four-inch leather knee-high boots were either going to get her killed or be ruined by the elements; either way, she wasn't really in the mood to deal with it.

Actually, if she were perfectly honest with herself, Monica wasn't in the mood for anything. Christmas had been the same as every year—a huge dinner at her parents' with a tableful of food and conversation she barely paid attention to. This year it had been highlighted by the two new additions to the family, one of which was Maxwell Donovan, who was almost ten years older than her youngest sister, Deena, but had married her anyway. Despite that slightly annoying fact, Max was related to the Donovans of Las Vegas, a family whose reputation for wealth, prestige and philanthropy preceded them.

The other addition was Samuel Desdune, private-investigator extraordinaire, who probably saved the gallery from a blistering scandal surrounding stolen artwork. Sam married Karena, moved her out of Manhattan to his country home in Connecticut and sliced her workweek almost in half. That pissed Monica off royally.

There was no way, not now or anytime in her future, that she would allow a man to dictate when and where she lived or worked. That was a simple fact. Monica took care of Monica; she didn't need anyone else.

Sam's family wasn't hurting for money, either. They'd made their fortune in restaurants. The Creole family seemed interesting enough. Sam's twin sister, Sabrina, was an ex-marine and now worked alongside Sam as a private investigator. Her husband was Lorenzo Bennett, a very talented sculptor—Monica was working on getting a few select pieces from him to show at the gallery.

All in all her sisters' choices of men weren't too bad, if you were looking for a man to settle down with. Which Monica definitely was not. No, settling down to Monica meant working even harder to open another Lakefield Galleries somewhere on the East Coast.

That's why she was here, with the wind chilling her right through her wool coat and sweater. That's why she was risking breaking her neck and ruining her boots to get to this cabin, to save Lakefield Galleries. Besides breathing, the gallery was Monica's first priority; its reputation and ultimate success were her only goals. Nothing and nobody else mattered.

Except family, she thought, lifting her hand to the knob on the wooden door with the sign hanging from a gold link chain that read Western. This snowbound-in-the-wilderness theme wasn't doing anything for her, but despite the fact that one of Monica's sisters was responsible for her being here, she loved her family dearly.

As she opened the door and took a step inside, Monica frowned. In addition to her job, her BlackBerry, her laptop and her family, Monica loved her high-rise condo in New York, where she lived comfortably alone.

Unfortunately, comfortably alone didn't look like something she'd achieve here. After stepping into the cabin, which was wall-to-wall wood paneling, Monica felt immediate warmth and slight trepidation. The warmth would be courtesy of the fire burning brightly in the fireplace taking up a good portion of the left wall. From another room she could hear the roar of a crowd, perhaps at a football game or something. A television was on and there was a black leather duffel bag on the peanut-butter-toned couch—hence the trepidation.

She flipped the receipt she still held in her hand and checked her cabin name once more. Western. It said it on the receipt and it said it on the outside of the cabin, plus the clerk had said "western cabin." Now, what were the odds that all three were wrong?

She let her purse slide from her shoulders, placing it on a long wood-and-brass sofa table. Thick, plush carpet muffled the sound of her heels as she walked through the area that looked like a living room, into a smaller room with a large-screen TV that displayed, as she'd thought, a football game.

"Hello?" she said, trying to elevate her voice over the sound of the television.

She didn't receive an answer.

Moving farther into what felt like a circular floor plan, she found a kitchen that was larger than the one in her condo with stainless-steel appliances, black marble countertops and dark wood cabinets. Very modern and almost spotless. *Almost,* she thought as her gaze settled on a glass half-filled with what looked like red wine.

Another doorway led her to a small hallway that broke off into two directions. She could see going one way would circle her right back to the living-room area and a view of the front door. In the other direction were two closed doors. She suspected a bedroom and bathroom.

By this point she was just about positive that either she was in the wrong cabin or someone had invaded hers. Feeling momentarily like Goldilocks in the home of the Three Bears, she took a tentative step toward the closed doors, yelling once more, "Hello?"

A few seconds later she heard the clicking of a door and stopped. Her mouth opened, about to announce her presence once more, then snapped shut when he walked out of the bathroom wearing only a towel around his waist.

Three days in the ski-resort capital of the world,— he could handle that. Despite what his brothers and his in-laws thought, Alex wasn't as focused on business as they complained. Okay, maybe he was, but that didn't mean he didn't know how to relax every once in a while. Besides, he ran a multimillion-dollar company, in the very competitive communications industry. He had to stay on top of his game at all times; that was the only way the Bennett name would stay top in its class. A goal he took very seriously, especially since it meant his father, Marvin, could finally retire with Alex's lovely mother, Beatriz.

Alexander Bennett came from a loyal and loving family with Brazilian roots that made them all the more passionate about any and everything they did. The oldest of three boys and two girls, Alex took on his role as a leader early in life. He worked alongside his father from his later years in high school all through college. Now, fifteen years later, he was the chief operating officer at Bennett Industries, second in line after his father, CEO Marvin Bennett.

Alex wasn't the only professional out of the Bennett children and he was very proud of his siblings' achievements. Although it had taken him a while to come around to understanding how serious his brother Renny was about being a sculptor, Rico's natural ascent into Bennett Industries' chief financial officer position was no surprise. His sisters, Adriana and Gabriella, both had their own goals, as well—what they were Alex wasn't entirely sure, but he loved them just the same.

But these next three days weren't about his family or his job—they were about having some fun. Renny's phone call had strongly advocated how much the men needed to get away, have some bonding time, especially since all the men closest to him had recently fallen into the marriage arena. Renny had been first, then through his in-laws, the Desdunes, Alex had sort of adopted Sam and Cole as his brothers, as well. Alex, Rico and Cole still remained single, but the poker nights they were used to sharing were quickly being cut to a minimum.

This trip was about them getting together and having a great time before the holidays ended and they all went back to their respective lives and businesses. And Alex was game for that.

Two days before Christmas he'd closed one of the company's biggest deals for a new line of cell phones with digital connections that would take them into the next century as a communications leader. The first of the year a number of articles would advertise their success as well as open the door for new stresses and headaches. What was the saying, "More money, more problems"? Alex firmly believed that was true. And while his ambition wasn't fueled by a lust for money, or power, for that matter, he wasn't naive about the facts of life. He was a rich man; his family was very successful and envied. And as they'd already experienced when they'd all been targeted by a jealous lunatic a few years ago, success could bring just as much bad news as good.

Still, he'd been raised to keep his eye on the prize and so he did. Today, the prize was looking better than he'd ever expected.

He'd just been turning off the shower when he heard a female voice. To say he was surprised was an understatement. Per Renny's instructions, the guys all had separate flights but would meet at the cabin tonight to get their getaway rolling. He'd arrived first, a little overeager, he surmised. Feeling the fatigue of the last few weeks' meetings, he'd come in and headed straight for a hot shower. To his knowledge this trip was only for the men.

Wrapping a towel around his waist he'd opened the door expecting maybe a housekeeper or some other resort employee to be in the cabin with questions or something. He'd never considered it would be her. Never in all his wildest imaginings thought he'd see her here.

But, he admitted eagerly, he wasn't regretting it at all.

Saying she was a vision in white would be corny. And Monica Lakefield was anything but. *Beautiful* didn't quite describe her, either—she seemed way too mature and regal for that word. But as she stood not three feet away from him, her face only momentarily wearing a look of utter shock before the cool chill slipped back into place, Alex knew he'd never seen another woman that affected him on this level.

This wasn't their first meeting. In fact, it was their fourth, and he'd have to say, as evidenced by the immediate heat simmering beneath his skin, the most enticing.

"Hello," he said, mimicking the greeting he'd just heard through the bathroom door.

Her brown eyes darkened just a bit, something he'd seen happen whenever he was close to her. With her flawless makeup, ivory slacks and matching turtleneck sweater visible through the opening of her long white winter coat, she looked like a winter queen. No, Alex corrected himself, an Ice Queen.

"What are you doing here?" The smoky timbre of her voice floated through the hallway and he took a step closer. Sure, he knew he was indecent, clad only in a towel, which in a minute was going to show the reaction he had to her each time they were close. But Alex didn't care. He was that way with women, sure of himself and of their reaction to him. He didn't think that made him arrogant, more like confident. The look in Monica's eyes said she didn't agree. But that only egged him on.

"I could ask you the same question."

Her gaze never faltered, never left his, even though

he knew she was well aware of his state of dress, or lack thereof.

"But that would be repetitive and waste both our time," she quipped.

He nodded. If there was one thing Alex loved it was an intelligent, confident black woman. The words seemed to personify Monica Lakefield.

"True. So I'll give in and answer your question. But you'll owe me." She opened her mouth to say something, a smart retort no doubt, but Alex stopped her by speaking again. "I'm meeting my brothers up here for a few days. Now, your turn."

"First, I don't owe you anything. Second, this is my cabin. I'm here on business."

"You're doing business during the holidays? Do you ever take a break?" He knew that had to sound strange coming from him, but in the grand scheme of things, he had the feeling he was nowhere near as ambitious and dedicated to his job as Monica.

"What I do with my time is no concern of yours," she said then took a deep breath.

It looked as if she had to force herself to let it out slowly. She was wound so tight she looked as if she'd explode in the next two seconds.

"Okay, just take a minute to calm down. I'm sure there's an explanation for this mix-up. Just let me get something on and we'll figure it out."

"Don't bother. I'll figure it out," she said then turned from him and walked toward the living room.

He'd bet she was heading for the phone, where she'd call her office to recheck the reservations, or to the front desk, where she'd interrogate the clerk as if he were a star witness in a murder investigation. For a second he thought about following her, trying to reason with her that it was probably just a mistake and nothing to get all huffy about. Then he thought better of that idea. Monica was not a woman to be calmed; that would only make her angrier. So he moved into the bedroom instead, taking his time slipping into jeans and a T-shirt.

When he emerged fully dressed and entered the living room, he wasn't at all surprised to see her pacing in front of the fireplace. Her dark hair was pulled back so tight he had a headache for her. One arm was at her side and the other was bent. A cell phone was in her hand, which she stared at, giving the device some choice words as she did.

He could stand here watching her for hours. She'd removed her coat so that he had a view of the formfitting sweater she wore and the perfect fit of the slacks. She was a tall woman, meeting him—at his six-foot-three-inch height—almost eye to eye with her heels on. Actually, they looked more like stilts and yet she moved gracefully with them, as if they, too, obeyed her every word.

"Any luck?" he asked when ogling her began to feel immature and obsessive.

"My phone's dead," she hissed, tossing him a heated glare over her shoulder.

A heated but very alluring glare, he noted.

"Let me see," he said, taking a step toward her and holding his hand out for the phone.

"You can't fix it," she accused.

"I don't know, me and a team of three designers just configured a state-of-the-art phone that will take us into the next century. I think I can look at a Black-Berry and see what the problem is."

With clenched teeth, she still hung tight to her cell phone. Until he reached over and, while one hand held hers with the phone in it, slowly peeled away one of her fingers at a time. He kept his gaze on hers the entire time because he sensed she liked to be in control, to keep what or who she deemed her enemy under close watch. When the phone was just sitting in the palm of her hand, Alex smiled and picked it up.

"I'm just going to look at the phone, Monica. Stop glaring at me like I'm going to ravage you."

"I don't know why but you give the impression of being smarter than that," she quipped.

Alex chuckled. This was more than a woman and more than a piece of work—she was one of those science fair projects that nobody signed up for because it looked too complicated and too hard to achieve any type of success.

Yes, she was definitely a challenge, and Alex loved a challenge.

Chapter 2

"It's dead," he confirmed. "Did you get the battery wet?"

Monica sighed. Not only did she not want to be here in this winter-wonderland town, she didn't want to be here with him. Of all the men, in all the world, why Alex Bennett?

"I dropped it in the snow," she admitted. "I can just use this phone." Moving to the small table near the couch, she picked up the phone and put it to her ear. There was no dial tone so she pushed the on/off button once, twice, still no dial tone.

"You've got to be kidding."

"What?" Alex asked from behind her.

Very close behind her.

He always did that, invaded her space. No matter where she was when he was around he made it his business to be only two steps away. It was annoying in a way she didn't want to explore. What she wanted to do was get as far away from him as she possibly could.

"The phone's dead. What kind of shabby place is this that their phones don't even work? When I get back to New York I'm going to kill Karena."

"I don't think the phone not working is any cause to kill your sister," he said in that deep voice that she suspected soothed and caressed every woman he ever met. Every woman except her.

"Don't tell me how to handle my sister."

"I wouldn't presume to tell you how to handle anyone, Monica."

And she hated when he said her name, hated the tickle of excitement it produced along the nape of her neck.

"Maybe they just haven't switched on the service yet. I've only been here about an hour," he said, putting a hand on her shoulder.

She put the phone down and stepped to the side, away from him and his all-too-knowing gaze. Another annoying thing he did was look at her that way. The way that said he knew exactly what she was thinking, how she was feeling. She hated it.

"Then I'll just get my things and head back to the main building. There has to be another room available since there seems to be some mix-up here."

"You can take a breath, Monica. I'm not going to assault you."

His tone held a bite to it that she'd heard before. Just as Alex Bennett always seemed to know what she was thinking, he also had a low tolerance for her. In fact, she wondered why he wasn't kicking her out the door. They obviously did not like each other.

"I didn't say you were going to assault me."

"Right. You're just acting like you're stuck in a cabin with a career criminal." He put the cell phone on the table. "Look, you just stay here. I'll go to the front desk and get another room."

He was about to leave her there alone, she was sure of that, when there was a knock at the door. They both stood still looking at each other for a few seconds, then Alex went to answer the door.

Monica sighed.

What was she doing? Being rude like she normally did. Well, that really wasn't true, she wasn't rude to everyone. Just men. Nobody had to tell her that she gave men a hard time—she knew she did. Especially good-looking, successful men that could possibly have some interest in her, or in this case probably couldn't stand her. Why did she go out of her way to be mean? Because she was smart enough not to repeat past mistakes.

Alex Bennett was a handsome man, with his dark smoldering eyes and burnt-orange complexion. He was tall, with broad shoulders and a swagger that said money and prestige. He commanded respect from the moment he entered a room, and he made the most adverse female's mouth water. She didn't want to acknowledge how attractive he was, but then again, Monica prided herself on being intelligent and candid. She called a spade a spade and as such had to say that Alex Bennett was one delectable specimen.

That's why she wanted to get away from him. He was temptation personified, and that she definitely did not need. Besides, this was a business trip. Wondering why he was here or just what he would have looked like had that towel slipped off was not a part of the deal. Those were thoughts she did not have time for.

"I've got good news and bad news," he said, startling her out of her thoughts.

She turned to face him. "What's going on?"

He had that half smile, half smirk that she never knew what to make of. Truth be told, she didn't know what to make of this good-looking businessman that could talk to her in an almost scornful tone one minute, then looked at her as if she were next in line on the dessert menu the next.

"That was the bellhop. He dropped off your bags," he said, nodding toward the hallway where he'd left her luggage.

"And?"

"And you were right, the phones are out."

She sighed.

"They're out because the storm that was forecasted to hit later tonight has already started. The winds have picked up substantially in the last hour, knocking out all power lines. It's probably done some damage to the nearest tower with a cell-phone signal, as well."

"Wait a minute," Monica said, holding up a hand as if that would stop the whirl of events as he was relaying them. "There's no phone and there's a storm coming."

He moved to the bay window and pulled the string that opened the custom-made blinds. "The storm's not coming. It's here."

Her heart sank like a seven-year-old's on Christmas who didn't see that Barbie town house she'd specifically requested. She stopped at the window, putting her hand up to the pane as if that would make the huge snowflakes blowing in the blustery wind any less real. "The storm's here."

"And," Alex said with exaggeration that drew her attention away from the true winter-wonderland display to rest solely on him.

"And what?"

He took a minute before answering, looking at her with those deep, dark eyes of his. "The resort's completely booked. We managed to get the last available cabin."

Her throat felt tight, as if maybe she was having an allergic reaction to something. "We?" she managed to croak.

"You and I are both on their records as sharing this cabin for the next three days."

"You've got to be kidding me," she said, taking a step back. "There must be some mistake."

Alex shook his head, his eyebrows knitting just a bit. "Something tells me this was no mistake, Monica."

He moved away from her to where he had his bags thrown on the couch. He grabbed one of the slimmer leather cases out of the pile, unzipped it and pulled out his laptop. In seconds he was punching keys, then waiting while the computer booted up.

"Renny called me Christmas Eve to suggest we all get together." He talked and pressed more buttons as she watched the computer screen. "When did you find out about the trip?"

Rubbing her now-throbbing temples, Monica thought about his question. "Karena called me Christmas evening after we'd all left my parents' house."

"Uh-huh," Alex said as he punched another button then looked up at her. "Just emailed Renny. He can't breathe without his phone so he checks his emails religiously. Hopefully, he'll answer in a few seconds."

"You can get internet connection?" she asked.

"It's probably not going to last long," he said, sitting back on the couch. "It's a little sluggish already. Before the end of the night we probably won't have much by way of communication."

"What?" As she folded her arms over her chest, Monica could do nothing but shake her head. "I can't believe this. I need to get another room. I need to make some calls."

"I think you need to sit down and take a deep breath," he said not bothering to look over at her. She could take that as him being rude but it was probably as much his personality as the bossiness, she was coming to realize.

"I'll just get my coat and head to the front desk."

"First," he said calmly, again not looking at her, "you'll probably get about five steps in that snow with those heels on. Second, there's no use trudging all the way up there when I just told you there are no rooms left."

She'd heard him say that before, but refused to believe it. Needed to refuse to believe it, was more like it. "That's ridiculous. This is a huge resort. How can they be totally booked?"

"Simple. It's the Christmas holiday. Lots of people who aren't into the big-family-gathering thing are very into the ski-till-you-drop celebration. Most of them probably want to spend the New Year here, as well. Let's face it, Queen, we're here for the duration."

He looked up at her then with a bleak expression.

"My name's Monica."

There was that half smile again as he shook his head. "Yes, I know. And, Monica, you might want to know that we've both been duped."

"What are you talking about now?" she asked with the last little bit of patience she had. How could this be happening to her? She was supposed to be meeting with clients, securing a showing at her gallery. How did she end up here with him?

"Renny just emailed me back."

"And what was his response?"

"I'll read it to you verbatim so you don't think I'm lying. 'Have a great time you two, LOL!'"

"What does that mean?" she asked, then realized she'd been asking this sort of question consistently for the past few minutes. Shaking her head she rephrased. "I don't understand what he's trying to say."

"He's admitting that they set us up."

She didn't even speak this time, just shook her head negatively.

"My guess is your sisters and my family got together and decided that putting us up in this cabin together would be a good idea."

"No," she whispered. "Not a good idea."

Alex shrugged, shutting down his computer. "I'm not saying I agree with them, but I'm not in the habit of whining about my conditions, either."

"I am not whining," she said with indignation.

Pushing the laptop into its case he chuckled. "Say that again."

"Forget this. I don't have to say anything" was her retort as she reached for her coat she'd finally taken off and thrown over the arm of one of the recliners.

She was in the hallway reaching for her bags when she heard his voice again.

"I already told you there are no other rooms and there's a blizzard out there. Are you really going to let stubborn pride get the best of you? I thought you were smarter than that."

With bag in hand and purse pushed onto her shoulder, Monica cast him a frosty glare. "I don't really care what you think about me, Mr. Bennett. Now, I'm leaving. I'll find someplace to stay for the night, then I'm heading back to New York in the morning."

She didn't wait for his response, didn't stay to see if he'd give her that half smile, half smirk again or if he'd physically try to stop her. Monica simply went to the door and jerked it open, feeling the slap of cold against her face as she did. Taking a deep breath, she stepped out into what he'd termed a blizzard and sighed. He was right—it was a blizzard. She could barely see two steps ahead let alone up the road to the building where the front desk was. Snow smacked into her face as she lifted her legs to take another step.

In the relatively short amount of time she'd been inside the cabin the snow had begun to pile up. There was at least a couple of inches sticking already and she attributed that to the mountainous region. She wasn't used to seeing this type of accumulation this quickly in the city. That didn't matter right about now. What mattered was getting away from Alex Bennett and finding out just what part her sisters had played in this scheme. With her next indignant step, Monica was fuming and ready to curse at the next person who happened to walk by. Instead the four-inch heel of her expensive leather boots twisted beneath her and a strangled yelp escaped her as her body and her bags plunged into the white abyss.

He'd stood in the door watching her walk away, watching the anger and pride carry her through the beginnings of a nasty snowstorm in bitterly cold temperatures. She didn't want to believe what he'd told her about there being no more rooms left—he shouldn't care. She'd silently rejected the thought that her sisters had set her up—again, it wasn't his concern. She didn't matter.

Until she fell.

Cursing, Alex darted out into the snow, not even aware that he had no coat on. She hadn't gotten that far so he reached her in no time. By then she was already struggling to stand on her own. Grabbing her beneath the knees and around the back, he lifted her up.

"Put me down. I can walk," she protested, squirming in his arms.

"Yeah, I saw how well you were managing that," he replied. Deciding to ignore the words coming out of her mouth now, Alex headed straight for the cabin. He deposited the seething, stubborn woman on the couch then turned back to go outside and get her bags.

When he returned she was standing right beside the door, hands on her hips, snow dripping from her eyelashes and the tip of her nose. She was angry and looked ready to spit fire at him when he took a step closer, cupping a hand over her mouth.

"You don't have to like it, but there are no other rooms in this resort. There's a storm just kicking up outside and it's freezing out there. I'm going to add some wood to this fire and see what we have in the kitchen because I'm starving. If you want to continue with this brilliant temper tantrum of yours, go right ahead. But I'll tell you right now, it's not going to change anything. I would take you for a smarter woman than to try and change the unchangeable."

After snatching his hand away from her mouth, Alex walked away, missing the choice words she mumbled, and headed straight to the kitchen.

Chapter 3

"I don't eat mayonnaise," she said when she entered the kitchen.

He didn't look up. "Fine."

She sighed. Eating crow was not an attribute listed on her résumé, either. Still, Monica knew futile actions when she saw them. She was stuck in this cabin, in the middle of a storm, with him. There was no way around it and rebelling against it was nothing short of stupid. He was right about that. And she was big enough to admit it.

"Thanks for coming out to get me," she said, moving to one of the cabinets above the sink, looking to see what was there. Two cabinets away she found bags of potato chips and took the barbecue and plain ones down.

"No problem," he said. "There are some bowls in that cabinet next to the refrigerator."

She moved in that direction, found the bowls and dumped both bags of chips into them. "These cabins don't usually come with fully stocked kitchens, do they?"

He was fixing sandwiches—ham-and-cheese from what she could see. The only condiment he had on the marble island counter was mayonnaise. So she decided to check in the refrigerator for something else. Or rather the low rumbling of her stomach decided it was time for her to suck it up and eat something.

"I think we can thank our meddling family members for the food, as well. There's enough in here to feed us for a week," he said as simply as if he were giving her the time of day.

After she found the mustard she moved to the counter to stand next to him. Not too close, but close enough. He pushed the tray with sandwiches on it toward her and she lifted the bread off one to squirt mustard on it.

He moved away from her then and for a minute Monica thought it was because she'd finally, totally turned him off. Not that she should care either way. The refrigerator door opened again and when she looked up Alex had two sodas stuck in the front pockets of his jeans.

"Bring the chips. We can eat in front of the fire," he said, taking the tray of sandwiches.

She followed without a word.

Monica thought they'd sit on the couch so she was surprised when Alex plopped down right on the carpeted floor in front of the fire and began tearing off paper towels. Shrugging, she again followed his lead, crossing her legs and sitting across from him. She even managed a small smile when he handed her a paper towel. She put the bowls next to the tray of sandwiches and accepted it.

"You want to bless our food?" he asked and sounded more sincere than she'd ever heard him before.

Momentarily speechless, she shook her head and he instantly began speaking a prayer. *Impressed* was an understatement.

"So how'd they get you up here?" Alex asked when he'd finished one sandwich and was working on his second.

She'd been taking small bites of hers because watching him was much more appealing. "Karena said she'd missed a conference call with one of the main sponsors of our Black History Exhibit. When I tried to call Bruce Mendleson back his secretary said he was here for the week so Karena booked me on the next flight out. I should have suspected something. Mendleson's secretary was too free with the information of his whereabouts. A good assistant doesn't give that information out to just anybody."

"And you're just anybody?"

"No, I'm not. But what I mean is unless I give my assistant permission to tell my whereabouts, she doesn't. All she'd say is I'm unavailable and she'll take a message."

"Have her trained just right, huh?"

There was a sting to his words but he looked as laid-back as if he were lounging in his own living room. Picturing him in the comfort of his own home was a bit disturbing. "Anyway, I didn't pick up on it right away because I was focused on saving the exhibit."

"You and Karena have been working with the gallery for years now. It's a great place. I've been there once or twice and my parents and their friends talk about it a lot. Both of you seem more than capable of doing a great job in the art world."

"Thanks." She sighed. "That's why keeping this connection with the Mendlesons was so important. After that close call with the stolen artwork from Brazil, I want everything to go as smoothly as possible. I need Karena to be more on point in her department."

"And you don't think she is? On point, I mean?"

"She's so focused on her new husband, their home and now this pregnancy. After she has this baby I don't think I'll see her at the gallery at all." And that was a fear she'd been harboring since the moment Karena announced she was having a baby.

"That bothers you. Why?"

"She has a job to do. She committed herself to the gallery long before she met Sam and his dogs," she said, peeling the crusts of her bread.

"Yeah." Alex smiled. "I've met Romeo and Juliet. Cute. Big, but really cute," he said referring to Sam and Karena's Great Danes. "But you know women can have a family and work."

He'd spoken so lightly, she figured so as not to offend her this time. Still, his words were as condescending as ever. This was the way their conversations always went. "I know women can do both, but not from a different state. Sooner or later the commute's going to hinder her ability to come into the gallery. I'm betting on that as soon as the baby is born."

"The commute's an hour away."

Pinching more off the bread than she wanted,

Monica wiped her fingers, now smeared with mustard, on the paper towel. "She used to live ten minutes from the gallery."

"How far away do you live?"

"Ten minutes."

He chuckled. "Is that the prerequisite for all employees?"

Chewing on a bite of her sandwich, she narrowed her eyes at him, seeing exactly where this line of questioning was going. "I hear you run a tight ship over at Bennett Industries, as well."

One of his thick, dark brows lifted in question or amusement, she couldn't tell. But the action had something in the pit of her stomach shifting, her thighs throbbing. She lifted her can of soda to take a big gulp. And prayed she didn't choke.

"Do you, now? Been researching me and my company?"

He grinned and that shifting went a little lower, resting in her center as she swallowed the last of her soda, wishing like hell it could quench whatever thirst was building inside her.

"No. Sam speaks very highly of you and your family. Although I don't know why he keeps telling me about you." She paused. "Wait a minute, you don't think—"

"That this was an elaborate setup to get us together? That's exactly what I told you earlier."

"That's ridiculous," she snapped. "And insulting. We're adults. If we wanted to get together we would have. We didn't ask for their little push." Her temper was steadily rising, heat infusing her cheeks even as her fingers clenched and unclenched. Then she noticed he wasn't saying a word. "Or did we?"

He looked momentarily confused, but Monica didn't believe that reaction one bit. Alexander Bennett did not confuse easily; he couldn't run a multimillion-dollar company with stocks as high as Bennett Industries' if he did.

"Did we what?" he asked.

"Did you know about this?"

His lips, a medium thickness with a dusting of mustache that fell neatly into the silky-looking goatee, thinned a bit before he spoke. "No. I didn't. Renny suggested we get away before we launched our new product the first of the year. And because I know how busy I'm going to be in the upcoming months, I took him up on the offer. Thought it would be nice to relax a bit after all the hard work me and the R&D team put into the Excel. Does that explanation satisfy you?"

"I just asked."

He'd begun cleaning up the space where he'd eaten and cast her a wary glance just before he stood.

"No, you accused and you suspected because that's how you are. You don't trust anybody because somebody betrayed you. It's a shame that for as beautiful and truly intelligent as you appear, you don't listen worth a damn."

Monica wasn't used to being spoken to in that firm and no-nonsense manner, even though she was quite comfortable using it herself. And she wasn't used to being walked out on, but Alex had done it twice. Actually, he'd done it at Deena's wedding and the first time they met at the gallery a year and a half ago. What really irked her was how well he walked away. Said what he had to say then left before she could rebut. Well, she had something to say, as well.

After scooping up her own mess, she went into the kitchen to dispose of it and knew he'd be there, as well.

"Look, I just asked you a simple question. Why you feel the need to dissect everything I say into some deeper meaning is out of my control. In fact, it's beginning to annoy me. You don't know me, Alex Bennet, and I don't know you. For whatever reason we're stuck in this cabin together. I think it's in our best interest to set the ground rules now."

"Ground rules?" he asked, turning to her.

He had just placed a bottle of water on the counter. As they'd discovered earlier, this kitchen was very well stocked, by a guilty group she'd deal with later. But for now, even the very attractive Alex Bennett wasn't going to change the uncomfortable situation.

"Yes, ground rules. You can have the living room and I'll take the bedroom. We'll stay out of each other's way until the storm passes and I can get another room. Deal?"

He stared at her for what seemed like forever, a look that had her shifting from one foot to another. Her nipples began to tingle—an action that coincided with the persistent pulsating in her center. It was stupid and basic, a punch of lust so hard and fast she could barely swallow after speaking. Furthermore, it was degrading to have such a physical reaction to a man that managed to annoy and slap at her each time he opened his mouth. But Monica wasn't a virgin nor was she a stranger to the urgings of a healthy sexual appetite. What she was not going to do was let any of that distract from the matter at hand.

Then he took a step toward her and her heart stuttered. Another step and the staggering thumping paused. She inhaled, trying to steady her breathing, and caught the scent of his cologne, or was it his body wash? Either was intoxicatingly sexy, male and enticing. Instinctively she took a step back, only to find herself stuck, backside against the counter.

He stood directly in front of her, moving forward until she had no choice but to lean back, tilting her neck to look up and keep eye contact with him. Eye contact was important—it meant they were on the same level, that she wasn't intimidated and that whatever he said or did she could handle. Which was a bunch of bull she fed herself about a millisecond before his lips descended upon hers.

Chapter 4

As kisses go, this one rated well beyond Monica's high standards. She struggled to figure out exactly where in the stratosphere it compared, then gave up and simply sank in. Wrapping her arms around his neck, pulling him closer, made it more a present pleasure than one just swirling around in her mind. Beneath her arms she felt the strength of his broad shoulders. Pressing against her with heated persistence, the delicious warmth of an aroused man. Her heart hammered as his tongue slipped fiercely into her mouth. He was consuming her, that's what she thought when coherent words surfaced. He was sucking and tasting, savoring and enticing. She was simply falling, falling until she didn't think she could feel the floor beneath her feet.

Then, as quickly as this pleasurable funnel cloud had swooped her up, it dropped her. Hot to cold, light to dark, beginning to end. Alex pulled back, stared down at her, then walked away.

Again.

About ten minutes ago she was ready to curse him up and down the snow-lined path outside the door for walking away from her. But right about now, it was all she could do to remain upright. Lifting shaking fingers to her still-throbbing lips, she braced herself, searched for her normal calm and prayed this momentary lapse hadn't just screwed up her plans of a peaceful existence in this cabin.

"That's not—" Her words were cut short when she walked into the empty living room. Where was he now?

Concluding it would be simply too embarrassing to go look for him just to tell him that little demonstration in the kitchen wasn't a part of the plan and that it wouldn't happen again, she stayed in the living room. She sat on the couch, figuring she'd just play it cool. If he didn't say anything about the kiss then neither would she. Although she was wondering what had made him do it.

Not five minutes later she could hear him coming again and sat up straighter.

"Now, about your ground rules," he was saying. He was carrying a box in his hand.

Trying to see what was in the box meant looking at him and she wasn't sure she could handle that, so she pretended to pick at a piece of lint on her pants. "They're simple—you stay in the living room and I'll stay in the bedroom." She stood and was about to get her bags and be the one making the grand exit, but he grabbed her wrist, stopping her.

"You can't just make the rules here, Queen," he said with a grin. "We'll have to play for the bedroom rights."

"What?" Asking him to repeat what he'd just said wasn't going to make her like it any better.

Then he moved his other arm, the one that had the box tucked beneath it. "We're going to play this game and whoever wins gets the bed."

"That is so juvenile," she said, then glanced at the box he was holding.

Twister.

"I am definitely not playing that with you."

"Scared?" he said, shaking the box so that the contents inside rattled.

Alex had made a grave mistake. A colossal error in judgment he wasn't sure he'd be able to overcome.

He'd kissed the Ice Queen.

And she'd kissed him right back. With a heated fervor that had him instantly wanting more, he might add. The first good thing that had come of the kiss was that he'd proven one notion to be true. Since the first day he'd seen her walk into Karena's office at the Lakefield Galleries there'd been this heat, this carefully banked inferno he'd sensed simmering just beneath her cool exterior. And damned if he didn't blow the top right off that assumption. She kissed like a woman full of desire and sensuality just waiting for the right man to caress it. But he wasn't that man. Or at least he didn't want to be.

Therein was his mistake. While he wanted to know what she tasted like, what she'd feel like in his arms, he was in no way prepared for the blast of desire that would rock him to his very core. In those few precious moments he'd literally felt consumed by her.

In business Alex knew to expect the unexpected and to always be prepared for new developments. In his personal life he sort of adopted the same rules. In the case of Monica Lakefield, he didn't really know which road to walk. Lightening the mood seemed to be the better idea.

When he'd first arrived at the cabin and had begun unpacking some of his things he'd come across the board games in the bedroom closet. Looking at the childhood favorites of his—Twister, Battleship and Sorry—had him thinking that maybe a family with children had stayed in the cabin before him and had forgotten their games. Fleetingly he'd thought the staff should have cleared them out before the next guest. But after the new developments of the afternoon he'd begun thinking that his family and Monica's had a droll sense of humor in their matchmaking scheme. Fill the kitchen with food and the closest with juvenile games—how that paved a road for seduction, Alex had no clue. Maybe it wasn't their intention for him to seduce Monica. Maybe they just really wanted both of them to take some time to relax and get away from their businesses. Monica would prefer to think the latter, he was sure.

The way she was looking at him now was proof that the last thing on her mind was seduction.

"Look, we have to pass the time or we're just going to drive each other crazy. I found some games in the closet and thought it might be fun." Her gaze kept going from the game box to his with growing agitation…and interest.

"Besides, you're the one who came up with the idea of ground rules. I don't think either one of us should just dictate what the other should do. So why not play for the bedroom rights? If you win, the bedroom's yours. If I win, it's mine. Simple."

One elegantly arched eyebrow lifted and Alex felt a tightening in his groin.

"Simple, huh?"

She was thinking about it, weighing the odds. He noticed she thought about things a lot, probably over-thought them. That either made her very careful or paranoid, both bringing him back to the conclusion that something had happened in her past to make her the way she was now. A natural fixer of all things wrong, as his siblings often accused him of being, Alex wanted to know what happened. He wanted to know more about Monica Lakefield, about why she'd built this enormous shield around herself and practically dared anyone to attempt to knock it down.

"Come on, Monica. You're not afraid of playing one game with me, are you?"

"I'm not afraid of anything" was her quick retort.

Just the words he'd expected to hear from her. "Great. Then kick off your boots and let's get started."

"I can't play dressed like this."

He looked at her pristine slacks and sweater and had to agree. "You go change and I'll get the game set up."

After a brief hesitation she said a quick, "Fine," and was out of the room before he could say another word.

Alex cleared the floor in the middle of the living-room area and spread out the giant plastic sheet filled with colored circles that would be their playing board. Then he looked down at his own jeans and shirt and thought he should probably change, too. As he remembered, Twister was a game of flexibility, which he wouldn't have much of in the constricting denim he was currently wearing. One of his bags was still in the bathroom so he grabbed a pair of gym shorts and slipped them on. He returned to the living room and his throat went dry when he saw her holding the cardboard dial that would instruct them throughout the game. It looked as if she'd put on gym clothes, as well—black spandex pants and a hot-pink top that just barely covered her midriff.

"What? I didn't pack any play clothes. This was a business trip, remember?" she asked, looking plenty guilty about her attire.

Guilt wasn't what Alex was feeling. *Hot* described it best.

"No complaints from me. But if you were planning to wear that to a business dinner I'd say you would be guaranteed to have all the pieces you wanted to show at the Black History Exhibit."

"Ha-ha," she scoffed. "Let's get this over with." She flicked the arrow on the dial. "Right foot yellow."

"Guess that look means I'm first," he said with a chuckle. She was beyond bossy. It was kind of attractive so he did as she said and put his right foot on a yellow circle.

"Right foot blue," she said.

"That's here next to me," Alex said, knowing she'd never stand that close to him. The kiss had rattled her, too, he knew from the way she'd remained quiet when it had concluded. Not that he'd stuck around to hear her comments, but if she had anything to say on the subject she certainly would have said it as soon as he'd come back into the room. Instead she had remained quiet about the situation, probably hoping her silence would make it go away.

It didn't. He felt the sexual pull to her stronger now than he had in the kitchen. The kiss had made the attraction to her all the more potent. He only hoped he'd have the good sense to keep his hands off her. At least for now.

She surprised him by placing her foot right next to his on the blue circle. He looked down, then up at her face.

"I don't like to be cold," she said, turning her attention back to the dial.

He wasn't going to say anything about her fuzzy black-and-white-striped socks. If nothing else they did look warm and she had packed to come to a ski resort. "I didn't say a word," he added with a smile.

For whatever reason she seemed awfully self-conscious about what she was wearing. In fact, he thought for a second, she seemed a little off balance since she'd changed out of her sleek Ice Queen outfit. Almost as if she didn't know how to act without the whole Monica Lakefield Businesswoman facade.

"Left foot green," she announced. Alex maneuvered himself until his left foot was on the green circle while his right was still on the yellow.

"Right hand blue," she said, then looked down at the mat.

"I'll do the spinning," he said, taking the dial from her hand. Her last bit of control.

She frowned at the loss then leaned forward and placed the palm of her hand in the center of a blue circle.

This put her in an interesting position as she'd turned her back to him so that now her bottom was strategically centered in his line of sight…and a nice bottom it was, he readily admitted.

After his next spin put him closer to her left ankle, which had found its home on a red circle, Alex's resolve against touching Monica again was melting. From the way she moved to one circle after another he could tell she was flexible, her long body limber and graceful. She probably worked out obsessively. That would be the only way she ever did things, he figured. Always to be the best. He wondered how long it would take her to figure out she'd most likely hit that mark years ago.

Without another word he wrapped his fingers around her ankle then moved his hand gently upward, stopping at her calf when she sucked in a breath and angled her head to stare at him. She didn't say a word so he let his fingers continue to walk up her leg, gliding along the satiny pattern of her pants before stopping at her inner thigh. Her gaze had gone all glossy then, her lips parted slightly. His own breathing grew faster as his fingers rested right there at the muscle of her thigh. Through the pants he swore he could feel her pulse thumping wildly at his touch. With a move so smooth and gentle it almost felt as if he'd practiced it, Alex repositioned both of them so that she was sprawled beneath him on the mat. Her heart was pounding, he felt it right up against his own as he looked down into her eyes. There was no fear there, not that he'd expected any. More like a question—a why and not a when—and he almost faltered.

No way was she wondering why he was making a move on her. She was an intelligent and confident woman—she knew damned well how sexy she was and that he'd been insanely attracted to her ever since the first day they met. She had to know.

Just like she had to feel his arousal throbbing fiercely for her now. Her lips parted farther and he thought she was going to say something, a protest maybe, or some smart retort that would shatter this mood. So instead of waiting for the cold water to be splashed on him, Alex plunged, taking her mouth in a kiss guaranteed to warm even the Ice Queen all the way to her toes.

Chapter 5

It was officially a lost cause. He wanted this woman, badly. And she, well, she wasn't putting up much of a fight. In fact, her arms had twined around his neck and her thighs trapped his between them as he deepened the kiss. He could take her right here, in front of the dwindling fire with the snowstorm raging outside. But he wouldn't.

This would not be a quick romp or a sudden release of the day's frustrations. When he took Monica Lakefield he wanted to take his time, to explore every nuance of this intriguing woman. It was going to take all the strength he could muster, but he wasn't having it any other way.

So Alex lifted his head slowly, delaying the parting of their lips for as long as possible. Breathing erratically, they stayed in that exact position, both with eyes closed for seconds that seemed to go on forever.

"I won," she said finally, her warm breath whispering over his face.

He wondered if she'd deal with this like she'd dealt with the last kiss—speak no evil, etc. Not sure how that thought made him feel, Alex opted for the cool comeback. "That's why I rewarded you," he said, opening his eyes to stare down at her.

She was not amused.

"My reward's the bedroom, as I recall the terms of our agreement." With that statement she used her palms to push at his shoulders, signaling him to get off her.

He thought about staying; clearly he outweighed her and could overpower her. But that wasn't his style, either. So instead, he shifted, rolling off her and watching as she quickly stood and rubbed her hands down her thighs. Thighs he'd felt flexing beneath him just seconds ago.

"I'll put your bags in the hallway," she said then turned to leave.

He could have gotten up, stopped her, made her address this attraction between them, but decided against it. He grabbed the plastic mat, doing some kind of folding job before stuffing it into its box. For anything to happen between them, Monica would have to want it; she would have to be on the same page as he was in her wants and desires. No way was he going to force himself on any woman, especially not this one. So tonight he'd sleep on the couch and convince himself that it was as comfortable as that king-size bed in the other room.

Monica hated the night.

Hated all the shadowed memories it held and replayed for her at will.

Taking a deep breath, she burrowed deeper under the comforter and closed her eyes, tighter than they had been before. Maybe if her eyes were closed tight the memories couldn't find their way inside her head. It was childish and probably sounded way beyond crazy, but this was her nightly ritual. All day long—from the time she woke up, usually at five, until the time her workday normally ended, around eight or nine in the evening—she was just fine. Nothing and/or nobody could throw her off her game. But the minute she changed into her nightclothes and sank into bed, the problems began.

Her past wasn't an easy one to forget. On most days she figured it was best not to forget—that way she wouldn't be likely to make the same mistakes twice. On other days she wished for something to come along and wipe her memory clear—like an IT tech would a hard drive. But Monica had no such luck, never did. Sometimes she wondered if she'd just been born in the wrong place at the wrong time.

That seemed awfully selfish considering the privileged upbringing she'd experienced. Her mother, Noreen Lakefield, came from a long line of strong black women in South Carolina, while her father, Paul Lakefield, came from an industrious family who'd made their mark in the steel industry. Her mother was the nurturer, there was no doubt about that. Anything that had to do with the three Lakefield girls was Noreen's business and hers alone. Paul rarely made time for the daughters he'd been saddled with despite his desires for sons. It was from that seed that a disconnect between Paul Lakefield and his daughters had grown. With Deena, the youngest, her father just had no patience at all. Then again, no one in the family really had a lot of patience for Deena's impulsive nature, though they'd all been shocked when she had invited them to her wedding last July. Monica was still getting used to the idea of her youngest sister now being a wife, a mother and published author.

The middle child, Karena, Paul tended to ignore completely. That sometimes happened with the middle child, and it had bothered Karena so much she'd taken it out on their mother. Now it seemed Karena and Noreen had reconciled while Karena and Paul came to their own terms of acceptance. It would seem that now it was Monica's turn, only she didn't want a turn. Her father was a taskmaster where she was concerned, always had been. As the oldest she was expected to be the strongest, the smartest, the best at everything she did. It was an unspoken doctrine that she subscribed to just the same. For years Monica struggled to make sure she did everything right in her father's eyes, everything acceptable. Her reward for those efforts was to never hear an angry word from Paul Lakefield about herself. That should have been enough, but not hearing an angry word equated to not hearing anything positive, either.

Sighing, Monica turned onto her other side, clutching the pillow between her arm and her head, pulling her knees up close to her chest. She felt like a child but noted the comfort and safety most children experienced was missing. Monica hadn't felt safe, ever. Comfortable? She didn't know the meaning of that word. To be comfortable to her somehow meant she was complacent, settling for things as they were, and she didn't want to do that. Not ever again.

She opened her eyes, tried staring at the ceiling because obviously keeping them closed wasn't blocking the memories out. Her heart clenched and she bit down on her bottom lip to keep from sighing again, or Lord forbid, whimpering. Show no weakness, another one of her mottos. If the enemy knew your weakness, he'd easily exploit it. Wasn't that what happened before?

Turning again, she realized it was useless. She wasn't going to get any rest tonight. At home she survived on about four hours' sleep each night. When she wasn't in her own bed, it was more like no hours' sleep. So, throwing back the covers, she sat up, pulling her knees up to rest her forehead on them. She was too damned old to be going through restless nights and harboring fears that couldn't possibly hurt her anymore.

If she were totally honest with herself she'd admit that her restlessness tonight wasn't entirely due to the haunting of her past. A very pleasant distraction was keeping her from sleeping, as well. And he was right down the hall, sleeping on the gorgeous but probably not-too-comfortable couch. But did he really expect for them to share a bed? They barely knew each other and she wouldn't even count the times they had met as getting to know one another. Then again, Monica didn't spend a lot of time trying to get to know anyone. It just wasn't worth it.

Kissing him was quickly becoming addictive. And Monica definitely did not do addictions. What she did do was own up to whatever issues she had. So she took a deep breath, lifted her head and stared toward the door. Alex Bennett was going to be an issue.

Finally tired of sitting in this strange bed, Monica stood, moving to one of the windows where she used her fingers to separate the blinds. They were room-darkening, and she needed some light. There wasn't much light outside, just the illumination coming from each cabin's front-door lantern. And through that illumination she saw the huge snowflakes that had splashed against her face earlier were still falling.

The mere thought of all that snow had her searching for her purse, digging through it to pull out her cell phone. That—her heart sank as she pushed the buttons—still did not work.

"Dammit!" she whispered and clenched her teeth. The minute she got back to New York she was going to the store to replace this stupid phone.

Maybe she'd buy one from Alex. Funny how her thoughts circled right back to him.

He seemed like a nice enough guy. A very shrewd businessman, which she'd already assessed from the way Sam talked about him. Besides, after their first meeting and the resulting connection between his family and the prince and princess of Pirata, which ultimately showed up at the gallery with a link to the stolen artwork, she'd researched his family and company.

Bennett Industries had made its mark in the telecommunications industry in the early nineties with their advancements in personal computers. While they were no Bill Gates, they did hold the patent to several programs and PC accessories that were used nationwide, including in the Pentagon, which was a huge boost in their stocks. For the past few years they'd concentrated a lot of effort in mobile devices and security communication systems. They had steadily growing stock and were featured in this month's *Infinity* magazine—a premiere publication owned by another branch of the Donovan clan—showcasing African-Americans on the move. The picture of Alexander Bennett sitting on the edge of his desk dressed in a black suit, white shirt and red tie was still fresh in her memory. Even from the glossy magazine page he'd touched her in that subtle yet potent way he always did. If she were really coming clean about everything she'd have to say she'd been attracted to him from day one.

It wasn't something she was proud of, physically wanting a man she didn't even know, but there it was. And just because she had this physical desire didn't mean she had to act on it. If they didn't keep bumping into each other, she wouldn't have to act on it, because she never intended to call him. But now, here they were. In a cabin, trapped in a snowstorm, ideal circumstances if she were thinking purely physical.

But she wasn't.

Although Deena would say she should. The not-so-subtle hints from her sister that she needed to get laid did not always fall on deaf ears. And while Monica certainly remembered the days when sex was as important to her as eating, lately that just wasn't the case. Until she'd met Alex.

It wasn't just his looks. Even though the dark, exotic look he had from his African-American and Brazilian heritage was reason enough for any woman to want him. For her it could never be just about looks. Alex was on her level. She could tell by the way he'd come the moment Sam had called him—family loyalty. Monica had that emblazoned in her brain. Good business sense and dedication to his job was another mark in his favor where she was concerned. It was important to take a job seriously enough to dedicate most—if not all—of your time to it. That, she told herself every day, was the true sign of success. The success of Bennett Industries was definitely a priority to Alex. He also didn't go out of his way to impress her; that was probably the biggest mark in his favor.

Just because she hadn't been in the mood for sex in a long while, didn't mean Monica had no clue about the men that were interested in her. She'd been approached more times than she could count, but they'd all tried too hard to impress either with their money or their status, neither of which she needed or wanted.

Tired of reminiscing and thinking she pulled on her robe and left the bedroom she'd played Twister so valiantly for. The other rooms of the cabin were dim, but she could still hear the low crackling of the fire in the living room. She did not turn in that direction; instead, she moved into the kitchen to find something to eat or drink that would help her sleep.

"Sleepwalking?"

She jumped, holding a hand to her now-thumping heart. Alex was standing in the doorway that led from the kitchen to what she now referred to as the den, where the television was located. Trying to act as if it was no big deal that he was there, watching her sneak into the kitchen, she opened the refrigerator.

"Getting something to drink if you don't mind."

"I don't," he said and sounded closer. Too close.

She surveyed every item in the refrigerator, not wanting any of them.

"See what you want?"

She looked up to see his face over the refrigerator door.

"Not yet. And you don't have to watch every move

I make. I'm perfectly capable of getting something to drink and going back to sleep."

She stood and slammed the refrigerator door.

"You can't go back to sleep if you weren't asleep in the first place."

How had he known? It didn't matter—the fact that he always acted as if he knew every damn thing that ran through her mind was quickly becoming the biggest mark in her "dislike" column for him.

"I'm going back to bed."

With a gentle hand he grasped her elbow and she stopped. "It's okay to admit you can't sleep, Monica. It doesn't make you weak."

Her back was to him so he couldn't possibly see the truth in her eyes, but he knew, no matter how, he just knew. She sighed.

"It's no big deal."

"Does it happen often? Or is it just because you're in a strange bed?"

"I think it's the bed."

He was quiet. She knew he didn't believe her.

"Would you like some company?"

"No!" She spun around to face him as she spoke. "Look, I don't know what crazy ideas you may have going on in your head. Just because we shared a couple of kisses does not mean I'm ready to hop into bed with you. Maybe you take sex lightly, but I don't. And I'm not sleeping with a man I hardly know!"

He didn't speak, but she heard him moving and wondered if he was once again leaving her standing alone. But the light came on and she saw him as he walked toward her. He wore only black boxer briefs that clung to the tops of his thighs and…his other parts like a second skin. His chest, as well as the rest of his sun-kissed body, was bare. Every inch of him was all male, hard contours, ridges and planes finely sculpted and well tuned. A feast for the eyes was the very least she could say to describe him. But Monica decided not speaking might be better. She tried to swallow instead, though even that was going to be a task.

"You know my name and where I work. If you'd like to know more all you have to do is say the word," he said as he came to stand in front of her. Then, cupping her chin and tilting her head upward so she was looking right into his eyes, he continued, "But don't mistake me for someone you once knew or someone you believe me to be. I wasn't offering to have sex with you. I was offering companionship to ease the jitters of being in a strange place. Yes or no is all you have to say."

And if she said no he would walk away. He'd go back into that living room and continue to listen to her tossing and turning in that bed just as he'd been doing for the past hour. And each time he'd heard her he'd stood, about to walk into the room to do what, he didn't know exactly. But the urge to do something was stronger than anything he'd ever felt before.

When he'd heard the bedroom door open he'd hoped she was coming back into the living room with him. But then he'd thought about the woman he was dealing with so he'd headed her off at the kitchen. She didn't want anything to eat or drink, Alex was sure of that. She wanted a distraction, something to get her mind off whatever was keeping her from sleeping. He'd offered her that.

She folded her arms over her chest, as smooth a protective measure as she could handle. She looked fierce and extremely sexy in the satiny robe that skimmed her knees and fuzzy socks he'd seen her in earlier. Her hair was loose, hanging down her back in a barely mustered state. Her cheeks were a little flushed, probably from her embarrassment about being unable to sleep. Why that would embarrass her, he didn't know. It seemed that any imperfection in her eyes was an embarrassment.

"I'll be fine," she said in a barely there voice.

"You'll be better with company. I'll just sit with you and talk until you fall asleep," he offered.

"Really? Will you read me a bedtime story and tuck me in?"

The sarcastic tone didn't escape him, but he took it as a defense mechanism and not a slap against him personally. "If that's what it takes."

She closed her eyes and lifted a hand to rub at her temples. "I guess we could talk for a little while."

Baby steps, he thought and resisted the smile that tugged at his lips. "Do you want something to drink before we head back?"

She shook her head. "No. I'm fine."

"Then I'll just turn out the lights and douse the fire, then I'll be back."

She nodded, turned and walked away.

Alex sighed and moved toward the living room. This getaway was turning out to be more work than if he'd stayed at the office. He would have to get Renny and the guys a special thank-you gift for setting this up.

Chapter 6

Monica sat up with pillows propped behind her on the bed and her hands folded in her lap. Her heart thumped in her chest as if she was waiting for someone to bring her bad news. He was coming into this room, with her, to keep her company.

It wasn't fear she felt, because just as she'd told him before, she wasn't afraid of him. Was she afraid of what could happen between them in this bedroom? No, she wasn't afraid of sex. So why was her heart pounding?

He entered the room, closing the door behind him, then silently walking around the bed to sit right next to her on the other side.

"You want to tell me what happened to make you not like falling asleep?"

At the sound of his question Monica knew exactly why her heart was pounding. He knew too much, things he shouldn't know. He saw too much, things she definitely did not want him to see. And he was usually right.

In an effort to not appear as neurotic as she felt, Monica released the breath she'd been holding in a slow, steady sigh. She could do this, she could sit on this bed and talk to this man without thinking another mistake was inevitable. Paranoia about men and their actions did not have to be a daily part of her life. If she told herself this over and over again maybe she'd believe it. Considering she'd been trying this for the past seven years and it had yet to work, she was loath to believe it now. And yet...

"It's not that I don't like falling asleep."

"Okay, then, what is it?"

"This isn't my bed, for one. It's not my home and you're here," she said and thought immediately that it sounded too harsh. "I mean, I'm used to being alone. And I know that I'm not now. I know you're just down the hall. It makes me a little uncomfortable."

"And now I'm right here in the bed next to you. Are you even more uncomfortable now?"

She thought about that for a minute and realized she really wasn't. "No. Not really. Don't ask me why because I can't explain it."

"That's fine. Everything doesn't always need to be explained." He crossed his legs at the ankles and turned his head to stare at her. "Why don't you tell me about yourself. Where did you go to college?"

Changing the subject was good, even though she would have still preferred the subject not be her. But at least he wasn't trying to figure out why she couldn't sleep anymore.

"I went to the University of South Carolina," she said simply.

"Really? I would have figured you for a Harvard or Yale type."

"I applied to all those schools and was accepted, but my mother is from South Carolina. She still has lots of family there, including a couple of professors at USC. I thought if I went I'd get a sense of some family history."

"And your parents agreed?"

"My mother was ecstatic. My father, well, he didn't really have much to say. I was getting out of the house and that was all that mattered to him."

"You make it sound like he didn't want you around."

She shrugged. "I don't think I knew what he wanted back then. Or now, for that matter."

"Not close to your dad?"

"Nobody's close to my father, except my mother. It's not that I don't see him, because he's at the gallery almost every day. But it's more like he's there to check and make sure I'm doing everything right instead of being there to see me."

"He doesn't trust you with the gallery? My brother Rico used to feel like my dad did that with him at our company."

"Really? So you're saying it's normal for a father to check up on their child constantly?"

"I don't know that it's normal. But I think it has more to do with their insecurities than the child's. Children naturally want to impress their parents, so they're going to go out of their way to do the job right. It's the parent who doesn't feel like they were doing a good enough job or that anyone else can do it as good as they can. That's usually the problem."

"Does your father go through this, too?"

"I don't think so, but then I'm not Rico. I don't work in the department where all the company's money is managed. My bottom line is to figure out how we can make more money. So I think I get a different measure of attention from my father."

"And you can handle that?"

"Sure. I'd be protective of my company, as well, if two hotshot young guys came sniffing around wanting to take over. But with your kids I think it should be different. There should be a level of trust there that doesn't exist with anyone else."

As she let her head fall back against the pillows, Monica could only hope. "I believe the same thing. Maybe you should try talking to Paul Lakefield."

"He's probably not that bad."

"You know what? I really wouldn't know how bad he is. I feel like I know so little about him. But what I do know is that the bar was automatically higher for me because I was the firstborn and the first girl."

"I'm the oldest, too. We do get a little more pressure than the others."

"At least you were a boy. My father struck out three times with all girls. I don't think he's ever gotten over that disappointment. So that made it even more difficult for me growing up. I always had to be the best, to perform the best. No slackers for Paul Lakefield even if you were a girl."

"Wow. Sounds tough."

"It was. That's why I couldn't wait to get out."

"And you did when you went to college."

"I did."

"And then what?"

She was quiet. He wanted her to continue, but she couldn't. They could talk about her father or her family or the gallery until the sun came up. But when it came to her college years, she'd rather keep that under lock and key.

"I think I'm sleepy now."

Very subtle, Alex thought. "Really?" There was a clock on the nightstand and he glanced at the time. "We've been talking for about forty minutes. I guess you could be tired now. Go ahead and get under the covers. I'll sit here until I'm sure you're asleep."

"You don't have to do that."

"I know I don't have to. I want to." And after saying the words Alex realized he really did want to sit right there and watch her sleep. He wanted to make sure she was all right and that nothing bothered her while she rested. So when she didn't hurry to move he started to pull on the comforter beneath her.

Reluctantly she lifted up so he could pull the comforter and sheets down, then she slipped between them. As he pulled them up to her chin, Alex couldn't resist the urge—he leaned forward, dropping a slow, soft kiss on her forehead. She was still staring up at him as he pulled back.

"Do you tuck all the women you know into bed with a forehead kiss at night?"

He smiled. "I'm not Santa Claus—I'd never be able to get to every one of them in one night."

She laughed at that. Really, her lips spread into a grin and laughter burst from her as if it surprised even her.

"Go to sleep," he said, warmed by the sound.

They lay in silence, Monica turned onto her side, back facing him and him just watching her. Her hair fanned behind her like a sheet of black silk. Carefully he lifted a few strands, let the soft tendrils run through his fingers. When her breathing steadied Alex relaxed against the pillows, turning so that he lay on his side, as well. They could have been mistaken for spooning, but his body wasn't touching hers. Still, he was close enough to feel her body heat. Close enough to inhale her scent. He wanted to pull her closer, to hold her in his arms and comfort her the way she really needed to be comforted, but he refrained. He knew better. She would come up swinging if he pushed her too fast. No, with Monica he definitely had to go slow. She'd given him a little bit by talking about her father, letting him see how she always felt inferior in the old man's eyes. That could be the reason she was so tenacious, so intense in her business endeavors.

But there was something else, something she wasn't telling him. Whatever it was, Alex knew it had to be the key to her fears, her reluctance to let herself go completely. He wanted to know, almost as much as he wanted to touch her right now. However, he would be patient. Patience, he knew, in the end would pay out.

In the dark of the night Monica shivered; it was so cold. Her nose felt frozen as she pulled the covers up closer, trying to create more heat beneath them. Her nipples tingled and hardened and her teeth chattered. But her backside was warm. For whatever reason there was some warmth back there. So she turned, settled onto her other side and felt the source of heat. Yearning for more, she moved closer and closer until she was enfolded in warmth. A sigh of contentment escaped her and she nuzzled even closer, loving the feeling of heat moving throughout her body.

She was in his arms, all soft and cuddly, her curves moving against his contours. And his hands explored.

They touched her shoulders, held her along her back, moved down to the succulent curve of her bottom, the line of her thigh. She sighed and he hardened. When his fingers gave up touching the silkiness of her nightgown and felt warm flesh, Alex almost growled. Lust tore through him in a primal rush and he lifted her thigh higher until her leg was wrapped securely around his waist.

She murmured something, her warm breath fanning over his neck, and he gritted his teeth. One hand slipped between her legs, sliding along the silken material of her panties to find the moist heat of her center. This is what was calling to him, beckoning him to come closer, press farther to find the hidden pleasure. He obeyed, pressing his fingers through the slickened folds of her center, feeling the warm wetness of her building desire, then finally, sliding sinuously into her honeyed cavern.

Her fingers clenched against his shoulders; her head fell back. His lips yearned for hers and he found them, thrusting his tongue quickly, deeply inside her mouth. Simultaneously his finger plunged deeper into her core until her coated walls clenched, locking him in place. The kiss was fevered, lips, tongue, teeth and moans. His finger inside her was dominant, wet, slick, deep, drowning. Her leg flexed around him as she kissed him with an unleashed hunger.

"Now," she whispered against his lips. "Take me now."

He heard her and then he didn't think he really had. He wanted her and she definitely wanted him. Take her, she'd said, practically begged. His body was doing some begging of its own as his own arousal poked persistently through the opening of his boxers. It took a moment's shifting.

"Please."

"One second, baby. One…sec—" The words were strained as he tried to move, to get them into the position he needed. Then he cursed, pulled his finger from the moistened pleasure to guide his own length to that same sweet spot.

The moment his tip touched there Alex cursed again. She sighed, thrusting her hips forward. "Yes. Yes!"

Her arms had slipped from his shoulders and wrapped awkwardly around his body until her palms were cupping the cheeks of his bottom. She pushed and thrust and through the slickness his erection slid into what felt as if it's one true home.

Chapter 7

The moment he was inside her his body relaxed, a sigh washing over him that confused as well as pleased. This was a new feeling, a new woman. Sensations Alex had never experienced moved through him even as he started to move with long, torturously slow strokes. She moved with him, her hands still pressing against his buttocks, both legs now lifted and riding along his hips.

He buried his face in her neck, inhaled the sweet erotic scent of her skin. The scent would stay with him forever, he knew. Just like the feel of her gripping him so tightly, the sound of her whispering her pleasure. This moment, this night, would be emblazoned in his memory and he would enjoy it immensely.

Nails raked along the skin of his bottom, upward to his lower back as her thrusts became more persistent.

"Please, more! More!" she whispered, her voice husky with desire.

Alex picked up the pace, always aiming to please. He lifted her legs until both ankles rested on his shoulders and thrust deeper, faster. He watched her, saw the exotic slanting of her eyes, the sway of her long tendrils of hair over the pillow, the tip of her tongue as it stroked her bottom lip just before she bit into it. She was an erotic beauty, desire and passion casting a glorious haze over her light skin.

He pushed the material of her nightgown up until plump, medium-size breasts were revealed, darkened nipples tight with arousal. Using this fingers, he tweaked each nipple, watching as her eyes darkened and her mouth opened wider to suck in more air. Inside she was so wet, so inviting that Alex almost lost his control. Every muscle in her body tightened as she moaned with her release. Alex thrust harder, searching for his own pleasure but didn't reach it until she yelled once more.

"Alex!"

His name was like a litany or a permission slip for him to let go finally. With a tensing of his spine, he groaned as it seemed everything he had inside was transferred to her. In a shameful display, he lay on top of her, breathing heavily and trying to find the ground on which he'd once stood, before he'd seen her in the kitchen, before he'd climbed into this bed with her, before she'd turned and wrapped her arms around him.

Monica was awake.

As much as she'd like to pretend otherwise, there was no denying it. She was coherent and Alex Ben-

nett, with his gloriously naked body, was lying on top
of her—a certain part of him still comingling with a
certain part of her.

She wanted to scream with embarrassment. The
woman who'd declared she would not have sex with a
man she hardly knew.

Then she wanted to sigh with contentment. The
woman who hadn't had sex in so long she feared she'd
forgotten how.

In the end she simply cleared her throat, then said,
"I need to get up."

"Oh. Yeah. Sorry," he said as if each separate word
were new to his vocabulary, and moved off her.

The chill air settled over her body and she shivered
as she stood from the bed. Her nightgown fell to its
original length, covering her naked lower half as she
headed for the door.

In the bathroom she looked at herself in the mirror.
Her cheeks were flushed, her eyes still a little dazed
with a mixture of sleep and satiation. She'd had sex
with Alex Bennett. She covered her face with both
hands, allowed herself a moment of bashing before
taking a deep breath.

"Okay. What's done is done. Get it together and
move on," she told herself then grabbed a washcloth
and switched on the water.

By the time she left the bathroom she was still giving
herself directions for how to behave when she entered
the bedroom again, what to say and what not to say to
Alex. He would be gloating and probably tossing her
words of not sleeping with him right back in her face.
It would be humiliating, but it was her own fault. She
didn't know what she was doing, didn't know they were

really doing it. It was a dream or at least that's how it had started for her. A private dream about getting closer to him. She didn't really want to get close to him. Or have sex with him, for that matter.

She stopped at the bedroom door and sighed.

She did want to have sex with him. She *did* want to get close to him. And it was fantastic. That was the biggest problem of them all.

"Congratulations," she said as she entered the bedroom.

Alex was sitting on the side of the bed, his boxers on but his chest still bare. He turned to face her. "What?"

"Congratulations, you proved me wrong," she said while heading for the side of the bed where she'd been sleeping before. "I think I'll be able to sleep just fine now. You can go back into the living room."

She'd climbed into bed and was pulling the sheets up over her when Alex stood. He'd lit a candle while she was in the bathroom so she could see his dark eyes growing even darker as he stared at her. She wanted to reach over to the nightstand and blow out the candle, but refrained. Her cool composure was only seconds away from faltering.

"Excuse me?"

Monica released a deep breath and looked down at the covers she was smoothing unnecessarily. "Thanks for your help, but I think I'll be okay getting to sleep now."

"Thanks for my help," he said with an angry edge to his tone. "I can go back into the living room now. You're dismissing me?"

"I didn't say it like that."

"You said it exactly like that. But just let me make

sure I'm clear. We kiss in the kitchen, you ignore it, don't mention it again. We kiss on the floor, again you act like it didn't happen. We make love and you—"

Monica's head snapped up at his words and she held a hand up to stop him from continuing. "We had sex. Let's not have any misunderstandings about what's going on. We had sex. It's done and we can't go back and undo it. Just like we can't undo the kisses. So there's nothing left to do but get some sleep."

Alex looked incredulous.

She sounded crazy. Monica knew this. She heard herself talking while a part of her sighed with disgust. Never in her life had she backed down from anything, especially not a man. Well, not like this. And she wouldn't have thought Alex could bring her to this point. On second thought, she did think that of him. Since their first meeting she'd sensed that he was different. And because of that her defenses toward him had to change. Obviously she hadn't done such a good job changing them.

"Now you want to sleep?"

She didn't bother to answer because her mouth could not be trusted to go along with her plan.

"Okay, that's fine. We'll sleep." He started walking as he spoke. "But I'm not going back in that living room. We've already 'had sex,' as you put it, so there's no fear in that department. I'm sure it won't happen again."

He was climbing into bed right beside her. Monica's heart beat a rhythmic jingle. "You can't be serious."

"Oh, trust me, Queen, I'm so damned serious." Punching the pillow beneath him, Alex rolled to his side, lay down and pulled the sheets up over his shoulders. "Blow out the candle. I'm not the one afraid of the dark."

Chapter 8

"Bree just called," Karena said to Deena through the phone; her sister and her husband had already returned to their home in Las Vegas. "Alex emailed Renny about Monica being there."

Deena cheered and Karena could hear the smile in her voice as she clapped her hands together and said, "Yaaay, they've made contact. So what else did Alex say?"

"Not much. Just that they're both at the cabin and Monica's not happy."

"No news there."

"Right," Karena agreed. "She's going to kill us when she gets back."

"Not if she gets laid while she's there."

Karena sighed. "Is that all you can think about?"

"Sure. Why not?"

"Deena, this is serious. We're interfering in her personal life. Doesn't that worry you at all?"

Deena sighed. "You're starting to sound like Sam. Look, Alex Bennett is a good guy. We're not trying to marry them off, just giving Monica a little push. She needs to relax and enjoy herself more. You know that. She's like a ticking time bomb, Karena. If we don't step in to stop her she's going to self-destruct."

"I know. I know. I just don't know if this little intervention we've plotted is going to work or come back to kick us in the butt."

"It's Monica, Karena, of course she's going to kick us in the butt. But if Alex Bennett's reputation is any indication maybe she'll go lightly on us on account of the supreme satisfaction she's gotten on this wintry vacation."

Only Deena could rationalize this situation in such a way. After hanging up the phone, Karena went back into the bedroom she and Sam shared. He was already asleep. As were Romeo and Juliet, who preferred their bedroom to the nice little room set up for them next to the kitchen. This was her family, she thought with a sigh, then touched a hand to her just-plumping belly. Soon she'd add an addition to that family and she couldn't be happier. Deena and Max were already beyond ecstatic with the adoption of the most adorable little girl she'd ever seen. Was it such a bad thing to want the same happiness for her big sister?

The day was brisk. Correction, it was biting cold in New York. He hated this city, hated the lights and all the people and traffic. His home was the South, where things moved at a slower pace and the rich had lineage and land to prove their status instead of condos and limousines and yearlong passes to everything showing on Broadway.

Yates Hinton was used to a much tamer lifestyle in Charleston, South Carolina. He had a house there on eighty acres of land, two cars and a thriving business. What he didn't have was the main reason for this visit to the city he despised.

Sitting in his hotel room, he watched the frigid air just about freeze against the windows as it blew. Even his coffee was now cold after only two sips. Thrumming his fingers on the table as he listened carefully to the report being read to him, he tried not to yell with impatience.

"So she's not here. Is that what you're telling me?" he asked the thin man with wire-rimmed glasses, beady little gray eyes and a mischievous smile.

"No. At the moment she is not."

"When will she return?"

"Her assistant wasn't sure."

"Wasn't sure or didn't want to tell you?"

He chuckled, a hollow sound that grated on Yates's nerves. He was paying this grinning idiot a ton of money to keep tabs on Monica Lakefield, to ensure that what Yates wanted he would soon get. So for now, he'd have to tolerate the slimy rat instead of wringing his greedy little neck the way he wanted to.

"Oh, she told me everything she knew. I can assure you that. But she doesn't know when Lakefield will be back. It was a last-minute trip. The plane ticket is open-ended. But here's the thing." He leaned forward on the table. "And this is going to cost you extra."

Yates leaned forward and stared into the fathomless eyes of this master extortionist. "Extra for what?"

His smile spread, thin lips moving over crocked teeth a shade or two shy of being white with one gleaming gold on the right side. "For the extra bombshell I'm about to drop into your lap. I think it's worth another twenty-five thousand."

Yates didn't even blink, as if the amount he was asking for didn't matter. "I need to know what the information is before I agree to pay for it."

"Nah, what if you back out once I tell you?"

"I don't have to tell you I'm a man of my word. You should already know that from our past dealings."

"Yeah," he said, contemplating Yates's words, rubbing a hand over his smooth-shaven chin. "You have been cool with your payments all this time. But that's because you were down south and needed eyes and ears here in the city. How long you planning on staying here anyway?"

"Don't get off the subject."

"Twenty-five thousand. Agreed?" he said, the smile gone, his business glare locked into place.

Through clenched teeth Yates answered, "Agreed." Just as Yates had been a man of his word, so had his informant over the past years. Sure, he'd paid him more than a high-school dropout could have ever hoped to make at a legal job, but up until now every report delivered to him had been worth it. He had no choice but to trust his instincts that this time it would be, as well.

"She's not alone on this last-minute trip."

Yates sat back in his chair, his hands falling to rest

on his thighs, the wool of his dress pants itching his palms. "Who is she with?"

"This is the part you're going to love. She's with Alexander Bennett. You know, the big cell phone and Galerite computer chip mogul. The room at the hotel is in both their names. Cozy, huh?"

He never ceased to amaze Yates. How a man of his limited intelligence knew about such things as the Galerite computer chip and the company that had introduced and patented the multimillion-dollar computer upgrade ten years ago, he didn't know. But the one thing he was right about was that this information was worth twenty-five thousand.

"I want you on a plane before day's end. Follow them and report to me daily."

He smiled. "And?"

Yates was already reaching for his cell phone. "I'll transfer the money to your account now."

"No problem, boss."

Chapter 9

Aspen

"Any news from the outside world?" Monica asked as she walked into the kitchen the next morning.

Alex had awakened first and headed to the bathroom before they could have another confrontation. One in which he most likely would have grabbed her by the shoulders in an attempt to shake some sense into her. The warm water had done wonders to calm most of the temper he'd harbored through the night hours. But he was still sore at the way she planned to dismiss what they'd done.

As he'd dressed, Alex had calmed even more. He'd decided he'd deal with Ms. Lakefield the same way he dealt with business deals. He'd take his time, map out his course of action, make note of all the weak spots, then move in for the kill. Or he could just let her have her way and move on.

Looking at her now, dressed in black slacks, patent-leather high heels and a gray sweater, Alex realized what he'd been trying to deny since the first time he'd met Monica—he cared about her. It was a swift connection from the very beginning, from the first chilly word she'd spoken to him and the spark of passion he'd seen in her eyes as she did. Everything from her cool exterior to her controlling personality and overprotective stance toward her sisters, ending with the vulnerability he saw the moment she realized they were trapped in the cabin. All of this made for one complicated package—one beautifully desirable, complicated package that tempted him sorely.

No, he wouldn't let Monica have her way. She wasn't walking away from him or what was brewing between them. Not if he had anything to say about it.

He shrugged in response to her question. "I guess no news is good news."

She moved past him, he guessed heading toward the freshly brewed coffee on the counter. "Good news would be that the phones are working and we can get another room today."

"You could at least fake it, you know."

"Fake what?" she asked as she filled a mug with coffee.

"Act like you're okay sharing this cabin with me. Pretend that this is a lovely winter getaway and relax enough to enjoy yourself."

She added only sugar to her coffee, then brought the cup of steaming liquid to her lips and took a slow sip.

"That wouldn't be realistic," she said, quietly bringing the cup down from her mouth.

"And realistic is running away from anything that's not on your agenda?"

"I don't have an agenda."

"Your whole life's been an agenda, Monica. Go to school, check. Get good grades, check. Go to college, check. Work at the gallery, check, check," he said, trying valiantly not to sound as angry as he felt.

"You don't know me," she said with a seething look.

He leaned back against the counter, folding his arms over his chest. "I know what I see. If there's something different you'd like me to draw my opinions from, than by all means please enlighten me."

She was clenching the coffee mug with both hands now, her fingers pressing so tight her knuckles were almost white. But that was the only signal that she was uncomfortable, that his words had touched her in any way. Otherwise, she was the ever-cool, ever-composed woman he'd met before. The one he now knew was a fake.

"I don't owe you any explanations."

"You don't? After last night you can really say that with a straight face?"

"Look," she said, her patience obviously slipping. "We're consenting adults. We had sex. So what? Get over it."

To say her words stung didn't quite explain it. Alex dragged a hand down his face and decided to take another approach. "Okay, I can get over sex. I'm a guy, after all. But not all sex results in pleasure. There was pleasure last night, wasn't there, Monica?"

She turned from him, putting the mug down on the

counter. "I'm not going to keep going over this. We really need to get another room," she said then tried to move past him in a hurry.

He grabbed her around the waist, pulled her so that her backside was to his front. And there was no question that in this position Alex was going to take full advantage of her and the unstable mood she seemed to be in. With his mouth close to her ear, he whispered, "You liked when I touched you here, didn't you?"

His palms moved from her waist to her breasts, squeezing the plumpness in his palms.

She sighed. "Physical reaction is easy, Alex. It doesn't mean anything."

"And you liked when I touched you here." One hand moved down, sliding past her belt buckle, down the zipper of her slacks to cup her center.

A hiss escaped her this time but she didn't move, didn't make any attempt to escape his grasp.

"Again, physical."

"But I touched you here, too," Alex whispered, his lips kissing her temple. "You were thinking about me touching you long before I actually did. You were dreaming about my hands on your breasts, between your legs. You wanted me even while you slept."

She could lie. But that wasn't her nature. She could avoid, which she was perfectly used to doing. But, Monica admitted to herself, she wasn't going to. Just because Alex thought he knew things about her, and actually did seem to hit some things dead-on, didn't mean she had to give in to him completely. It was obvious that he wanted this physical relationship between them. It was simple enough, she surmised. Anything else would be too complicated, too difficult for her to even consider. But this—the feel of his hands on her, his lips on her, the shimmer of heat that moved throughout her body when he talked to her in this tone—she could enjoy this.

"I don't doubt there's a physical attraction between us. I wanted you and you wanted me."

"Do you want me now?" he asked, nipping her earlobe. "When you woke up this morning did you wish I was still lying there next to you? Did you want me to come inside you again? Tell me, Monica. Tell me you still want me."

Again, lying would be futile. She did want him. Again. And why shouldn't she have him? There was no real issue stopping them from having sex, as long as that's all they did.

"Yes," she answered finally and let her body melt back into his.

He startled her with his next move. Turning her so fast she literally felt as if the room was spinning and lifting her up off the floor. She gasped when he set her on the countertop they'd just been leaning again.

"What—" She opened her mouth to speak but he moved faster.

His lips barely touched hers as his tongue took full advantage, reaching inside to meet hers in a heated duel that made her center pulsate.

"Don't talk," he said, dragging his lips from hers, his teeth raking over her cheek, across her jaw. "Just feel."

Oh, she was feeling, all right. Feeling dizzy, aroused, hot, anxious and a bunch of other words that were lost to her right now. Every physical reaction moved through her like its own private storm, filling her body with a tumultuous yearning she was sure she'd never felt before.

"Let yourself feel everything I do to you. Don't analyze it—just let it be."

Flattening her palms against the counter, she leaned back as his tongue trailed a heated path down her neck to her collarbone. Her breasts tingled, felt full and achy. They needed to be touched, wanted to be suckled. She arched her back and offered them to him, and he quickly accepted her offer. Deft fingers released each tiny button down the center of her sweater in record time. With what seemed like a magical flick of his wrist he unhooked the front clasp of her bra, and when her needy breasts sprang free he cupped one in his palm while taking the other's plump nipple into his mouth.

The whoosh of air she sucked in too quickly filled her lungs then came gushing out with a strangled moan. Her teeth sank into her bottom lip as she shifted her bottom, trying desperately to alleviate herself of some of the building need.

His mouth seemed designed to punish today, raking teeth down her rib cage, over her stomach, stopping when his tongue dipped inside her navel. She was arched completely back, bowed like a ballet dancer on the kitchen counter, when his quick fingers flipped the button on her pants. Without direction Monica lifted her hips, allowed him to push the pants and her panties down until they stopped at her ankles. She toed her shoes off and sighed when the pants and undergarments hit the floor.

"That's it, Queen, give me everything you've got," he whispered as his hands pushed her thighs apart.

For an instant she felt brazen, like a temptress offering her wares. And he, Alex, the bronzed god that seemed infatuated with her body, looking down at her as if she was a feast for the taking.

That thought made her body hum all over. She moaned. He made a sound that reminded her of a growl, a primal sound that had her heart flip-flopping in her chest.

He touched her first, his fingers exploring her most secret part. Warmth washed over her plumped folds as he leaned closer, whispered something over her before dropping small kisses up, down, all over her aching center. Her nails scraped over the marble counter that had now grown as warm as her body.

When his tongue made one long stroke from the top of her juncture to the center Monica felt as if liquid fire now coursed through her veins. If she bit down on her lip any harder she'd definitely draw blood. Instead she opened her mouth slightly, tried to breathe as normally as she possibly could without hyperventilating. But it was a futile effort. Alex acted as if she were the most delectable meal he'd ever tasted. Every stroke was followed by a moan from him, his fingers moving over her with touches as light as a feather, sparking licks of heat up and down her spine.

His name tumbled from her lips. "Alex." It sounded like a plea and she instantly wished she could take it back.

Strong hands moved to her thighs, lifting them slightly off the counter and pulling her closer to the edge, his tongue slipping deeper inside her. Her hips moved, worked in the same glorious circular motion as his mouth. Her head fell back, breath coming in fast pants, coherent thoughts flitting through her mind like a foreign memory. Her hands itched to grab the back of his head, to guide his motions to fit her growing need. She refrained and felt the twisting feeling of being lifted higher and higher. So high that when she finally fell it was as if she'd jumped from a cliff into the clouds and with breathless pleasure Monica sighed his name again—this time not feeling a moment's trepidation.

Chapter 10

"I didn't protect you last night," Alex said, standing up straight between her legs. "I apologize. It won't happen again."

He was talking. She could hear him but wasn't a hundred-percent sure what he was saying. Her thighs were still shaking, her nipples almost burning with need. Lifting her head she looked at him, saw that he was quickly undoing the button of his own pants and pushing them and his boxers down past his hips. Where it came from she'd never know, but he ripped a condom package open with his teeth then hastily donned the latex. The second she opened her mouth to speak, he thrust his length inside her and she swallowed whatever she was going to say.

This was different from last night, his strokes more fevered, moving inside her like a man with a mission. A mission to disperse as much pleasure on her as he possibly could, she figured. Well, he'd already done a good job of that. She wrapped her legs around his waist, her arms around his shoulders and let him take her higher again and again.

He wanted her to feel and she was doing exactly that. Feeling every thrust of his pelvis, every stroke of his tongue over her lips, her neck, with the sensitivity of a seasoned lover. This was exactly how she'd always thought it should feel, how sex should be between a man and a woman. It was everything she'd dreamed of but dared not believe possible.

No, it wasn't the romance of the century—they were having sex on the kitchen counter, after all—but it was something. It was something much more than she'd ever thought she'd experience. And no matter how much Alex Bennett could annoy her, she'd have to give him props for being so skilled in this area.

These were coherent thoughts; they were analytical, the norm for Monica. And so out of place right now it took him lifting her completely off the counter, holding her around him as his length plunged deeper and deeper into her center, to wash all those thoughts away.

Their release came simultaneously this time. She could tell by the way he held her tighter, the guttural moans and raspy way he said her name, just as her thighs tightened around him, spasms of pleasure vibrating throughout her body.

"I can run my own bath," she protested even though the water was already run, fluffy bubbles all but dripping over the rim.

Alex had carried her into the bathroom, set her on

the closed toilet seat and dared her to move. She'd obliged but he knew that was because she was still riding the euphoric wave of her release. He had to admit his legs were still a little shaky from his own release, but he wasn't about to show her that.

"Do you ever stop arguing?" he asked, switching off the water and pulling his shirt over his head.

"I'm not arguing. Just stating a fact."

He moved to her then, pulling her sweater from her arms and removing the bra that dangled beneath. "I ran us both a bath and now we're going to enjoy it." He removed her socks then lifted her up into his arms.

"You're bossy," she said but didn't try to get out of his grasp.

"I've heard that before."

Alex set her down into the water and watched with amazement as the questioning look on her face dissipated. She took a deep breath, exhaled then prepared to lay back against the lip of the tub.

"Not so fast," he said then climbed in.

Water sloshed and bubbles did make their way to the floor as he positioned himself behind her, pulling her back so that her head rested on his shoulders, bubbles reaching up to just cover her breasts.

"I don't bathe with men," she said, but she leaned into him just the same.

"Then let me call the police now because it looks like that's just what you're doing."

"You can't control me." Her voice was light, without the conviction she had when he knew she really meant business. In fact, she'd lifted a hand and was now cupping bubbles, bringing them to her face to blow them.

"Never thought I could. But I can enjoy you."

He could also begin to really enjoy holding her naked body against him, but wasn't going to bring that up just yet.

"You like bubble baths?"

She shrugged. "It's one of my favorite indulgences."

"It's nice to know you take the time to indulge yourself."

"I'm not as uptight as you may think. I know how to make myself feel important. It's a necessity for women in this day and age."

"What's that supposed to mean?"

"Just that we have to be able to please and appreciate ourselves instead of always waiting for a man to do it. Then we won't be so disappointed when men do one of the things they do best, forget."

And if that didn't speak volumes about the humongous chip she carried on her shoulder, Alex didn't know what did.

"Some men know how to appreciate, as well as please, a woman. But I don't see any harm in a woman taking responsibility for her own satisfaction. Who would know best what pleases you than yourself?"

"Exactly. And this way I'll always be pleased with the outcome."

He let those words linger in the air a moment. "You haven't been pleased much, have you?"

She was silent. "I don't look for pleasure anymore."

Her words were spoken softly and she'd stopped blowing the bubbles. Now she flattened her palms over them, pushing them away from her body. It wasn't a terribly important motion, nothing for him to watch and contemplate. But he did. As a child Alex loved to put together puzzles, loved finding the pieces that fit and watching the completion of a job well-done in the end.

Monica had several pieces of herself that she thought she was doing a really good job keeping out of the public eye, but Alex saw them. Better than that, he could hear the different pieces in Monica the more he talked to her. Even if her answers were sometimes curt, or purposely obtuse, he knew there was something deeper, something really bothering her.

"Then maybe you should just enjoy it when it's offered," he said, lifting a cloud of bubbles in his palms and bringing them up to her face.

She stiffened against him instantly and he slowed his motions, caressing the bubbles along her cheeks, down her neck and over her shoulders until he felt her relaxing again. She'd thought he was going to smear them in her face, a joke of sorts, but he knew her better than to attempt that. The key to Monica Lakefield, he'd discovered, was to keep her guessing. If she could anticipate your next move, she'd be ready to counter it. But if she didn't know what to expect, she might actually accept what he was trying to give her.

What that was, Alex wasn't really trying to confirm right now. He was simply going with his gut, something he'd always done that had rarely let him down.

"How many women have you seduced in the bathtub?" she asked.

"Hmm, let me see," he joked but noted she shifted against him as if she were uncomfortable with his impending answer. "None," he continued seriously.

"You want me to believe you've never bathed with a female before?"

"What I want you to do is trust that when you ask me

something I'll give you nothing but an honest answer. I'm not a man that plays games, Monica. What you see is what you get with me."

She sighed. "That's different."

"You're different," he said. "That's why you are the first woman I've ever taken a bubble bath with."

Monica moved again then berated herself for making that same mistake in such a short span of time. Moving only rubbed her back against his hard chest, had his thick erection moving like heated silk over the lower part of her back and just overall made her hunger for him once more. It was a silly mistake that her body kept making without her mind's input.

And to top that off she was talking too damned much. He didn't need to know what she looked for in a man, didn't need to know the personal whys and hows of her life. That wasn't what this was about. It was about two adults slaking a need. Period.

With that settled in her mind she reached for the soap, sitting up so she could wash and get out.

"You ready to get out so soon?" he asked in that voice that seemed to have gone a couple octaves deeper since they'd come into this bathroom.

This shouldn't be a romantic spot; it shouldn't have her feeling all mushy inside because he thought enough about her after their heated round of sex in the kitchen to run a hot bath and to add bubbles—which was really one of her all-time favorite relaxation methods. But that didn't matter. He shouldn't have done it, but he did and now she was confused all over again.

"The water's getting cold." A lie. Now he had her lying to him and to herself. She wanted to scream.

Chapter 11

Monica's free speech with Alex continued throughout the day. They moved about the cabin as if this were a planned lovers' getaway. He was always in the same room she was, and since the electricity was still out they had no choice but to talk.

There was something to be said for talking, Monica thought now as she changed into a nightgown and prepared to go to bed for the night. She'd learned things about Alex Bennett she hadn't known before. Not that she knew all that much about him. More like she knew of his family but not about him, the man. What she'd learned surprised her and had her looking at him a little differently thann she had before they'd been stranded here together. Or maybe that was the sex talking; maybe she saw him differently because she knew him intimately now. Either way, she wondered how they'd go back to their normal lives after this.

Alex Bennett was not the pampered rich professional she'd first thought him to be. She'd learned that he was a very loyal and compassionate man who loved his family beyond anything else. He respected both his parents and treated his siblings as if they were his own children. She suspected his siblings didn't really like that side of him, but as the oldest child herself Monica could certainly relate to feeling responsible for them.

He said he didn't lie. She still found that hard to believe, yet everything he'd told her today stuck in her head like sales figures or projected profits.

Business was only his second love; his first was family. "I'd like to get married and have a family one day. Probably not as soon as my family and friends would like me to, but I'm definitely headed in that direction."

"Really? Do you have the wife and the house all picked out, too?" she'd asked before her mind could censor the tone of her question. Yet something about the way he'd stated so matter-of-factly his plans for the future had her bristling.

Alex had only chuckled. "No, that's what's taking me so long. She has to be the right woman."

"Ah, the perfect-woman search. I wonder how long you'll have to look."

He didn't touch her but his gaze sent shivers down her spine as he zeroed in on her. "Not the 'perfect' woman. I said the 'right' woman. There's a difference."

She'd shrugged, hoping the unfamiliar feeling coursing through her at the moment would pass. It didn't matter which woman Alex Bennett was searching for, she definitely was not the one. And didn't want to be.

* * *

Monica was speechless, a new state of being for her. But when she walked into the living room, lit by only the warm orange glow of the fireplace, she couldn't speak. They'd been using candles since the electricity went out yesterday so seeing them didn't automatically suggest romance. But this roaring fire in the center of the big living area, a blanket spread out in front of it with a bucket and bottle of wine, did make her think romance. Moreover, it made her think this thing between her and Alex was going somewhere she didn't want it to go.

"I thought we were going to bed," she said, clearing her throat.

"Come and sit down for a few minutes." He motioned her over.

He still wore the sweats he'd had on all day with the T-shirt that shouldn't be sexy but most definitely was. Something about the way the firelight danced over his creamy caramel complexion made her nipples ache. His dark eyes now held flecks of light, the muscles in his arms were more pronounced, his glare seemingly hungrier. It was crazy, she thought, standing here worried about taking a step toward him. She was a grown damn woman; she had nothing to be afraid of.

"Have a drink with me," he stated when she was kneeling onto the blanket.

"You didn't have to do all this." She didn't want him romancing her, or trying to get closer to her, for that matter. Considering they'd had sex a couple of times now and were still trapped in this cabin together, closeness probably couldn't be prevented. But there was no sense in creating something that wasn't there, or rather, couldn't be there.

"I did it because I wanted to, Queen. Stop over-analyzing everything I do like you can figure out what my next move is."

"That's not what I'm trying to do."

His answer was a lift of his eyebrow and Monica simply sighed.

"Okay, fine. I'll have a drink with you, then I'm going to bed. I'm sleepy."

"Really?" he asked. "Are you often tired before you go to bed then stalled for sleep when you get there?"

She'd almost forgotten he knew about her insomnia now. Another slip on her part. It seemed where Alex Bennett was concerned Monica was doing a lot of slipping.

"I get tired just like everyone else. Even though we haven't done much today in the confines of this cabin, I still feel like I could lie down and get some rest."

"What happens when the memories come back?"

No, she was not going to go there with him. Telling him about her past would undoubtedly open a door he'd never want to close. And that was not an option.

"I know how to deal with my life, Alex." She took a deep breath, looked around the darkened room and felt the warmth from the fire ripple along her skin. "Why do you always think you can save everybody, fix everybody?" she asked. "You told me earlier about your sisters and how you help them out of scrapes all the time. Why do you do that?"

"I don't like to see the people I love and care about hurt or in trouble. If there's something I can do to prevent that or to make their lives easier, I do it. Don't you do the same for your sisters?"

Monica shook her head. "I believe everyone can learn from their mistakes. If I prevent Karena and Deena's mistakes then what will they learn? How will they grow into better women?"

"And you think they can be better women? Better in what respect, until they're acting like you?"

"I don't want anybody to act like me, nor do I wish any of what I've gone through on anyone. I just want them to make intelligent decisions, to live the life they want to lead to the fullest."

"With your approval, of course?" he asked with a tilt of his lips. "You didn't want Karena to marry Sam and you didn't want Deena to marry Max."

"I don't think they need a man to define them. Would you want your sisters getting married just because they thought they couldn't live without a man?"

Now Alex chuckled. "Gabriella's twenty-five—she's my baby sister. Do I personally think she's ready for the commitment of marriage? No. But if she meets a man and falls madly in love with him, I'm not going to be the one discouraging her from following her heart. I will, however, threaten to break the dude's kneecaps if he even thinks about hurting her."

Monica had to smile at that. "I've made that threat before."

"I'll just bet you have, Queen." Alex laughed with her. "Now, Adriana, she's twenty-seven and much more mature than Gabriella. She's sort of figured out that her modeling days are over and is looking into some type of management, taking some courses in college to gain more knowledge of the other side of the entertainment industry. I admire her for that. Any man that wants Adriana's heart will have to know her soul first. So when she says she's ready to get married, I'll know it's the real deal."

"And you'll threaten this man's kneecaps, as well?" Her mood had begun to lighten. Talking to Alex did that to her. *He could be a friend,* she thought distantly. If she allowed herself to have friends.

"That goes with the big-brother territory. Besides, Rico and Renny do a lot of threatening, too. I'm not taking that charge by myself."

Monica found herself laughing again and beginning to like this man way too much.

Alex loved her laugh and thought her smile had to be a slice of heaven.

Tonight she wore cream-colored leggings that looked like silk running up and down her legs. Her shirt was long enough to cover the curve of her bottom but still hugged the plumpness tightly. He'd swallowed hard when she came into the room, then he'd looked into her eyes.

So many questions still remained, so much trepidation. He wanted to wipe it all away with a kiss or a hug or lovemaking that would erase any thoughts of her past, but Alex knew that wouldn't work. He could do all those things, surely, but that would just be a temporary fix, a bandage for a cut that most likely needed stitches.

As she settled herself onto the blanket, at what she probably thought was a safe distance from where he sat, he shifted, pretending to stoke the fire. "Pour us a glass," he said over his shoulder before her mellow mood turned defensive again.

While she was pouring he finished with the poker and settled back, scooting over closer to her. When she turned with a glass in each hand she was surprised to see him right there. He simply smiled and took a glass from her hand.

"A toast," he said before she could protest. "To a great cabin, a big blizzard and to both of us knowing how to bust someone's kneecaps."

Her smile was a little more hesitant this time, the corners of her lips trembling in a motion that warmed him more than the fire. Lifting her glass, she toasted. Then she added, "And to the lights coming back on and the roads clearing."

The mellow was quickly wearing off. "I'll toast to that even though it hasn't happened yet."

"Wishful thinking," she said before taking a sip.

"You're still trying to run from me? I would have never pegged you for a runner."

Something flashed in her eyes after he spoke but everything else about her remained cool. She took another sip and lowered the glass to sit on the floor. "I don't run from anybody."

He nodded. "You just steer clear of any problems or any unsightly entanglements."

"I protect myself at all costs."

"And you've been doing that how long, Queen? Since he hurt you?"

She shook her head. "We're not doing this." She moved to get up but Alex reached for her, wrapped his arms around her waist and pulled her to him. They were both on their knees now, staring into each other's eyes.

"He didn't do anything I didn't allow him to do," she said finally.

"That doesn't mean whatever he did was right," Alex retorted.

Monica shook her head. "It doesn't matter. It's in the past. And I don't want to talk about it," she said with finality.

"At some point in our lives, we all do things we don't want to do."

"Not me. Not anymore." Her lips set firmly as she looked away from him, her dark eyes focusing on the crackling fire.

Alex touched a hand to her chin, turned her face so she was looking at him again.

"I cannot apologize for whatever he did or didn't do. All I can do is promise I won't make the same mistake."

"How can you say that when you don't know what he did?"

"Because while I may be a lot of things, Queen, I'm no fool." He traced a finger over her bottom lip. "And only a fool would do something to hurt you."

It was ridiculously silly for her insides to turn to mush at his words, not to mention naive. But Monica couldn't fight the feeling. She couldn't resist the urge to move closer, to let him take her in his embrace, to be held and comforted, for once. And when Alex did just that she knew she was a goner.

Chapter 12

Connecticut

"It's been two days," Karena said with a sigh.

"They're fine, baby." Sam kneaded her shoulders then moved down to her back.

"No, they're not. Alex's probably dead and stuffed in a closet by now. Monica does not have a high tolerance level."

Sam chuckled. "She's not a murderer, either."

"Whatever. You laugh if you want, but something's definitely going on up there and I don't think it's good."

Before Sam could reply Karena's cell phone rang. He scooped it off the coffee table and handed it to her.

"Karena Desdune," she answered. It was the ringtone of a business call.

"Mrs. Desdune, this is Adonna from the gallery."

"Yes. Adonna, how can I help you?" She wasn't sure why Monica's assistant was calling her but it couldn't be a good thing.

"I'm trying to get in touch with Ms. Lakefield. I have an urgent message for her as well as a package that arrived yesterday morning. I've been calling her cell and emailing her but I'm not getting any response. I thought she'd be back in town by now so I figured I'd give you a call to see if you could advise what I should do."

Adonna Banks did whatever Monica instructed her to do. She'd been Monica's assistant for the past five years and knew her job inside and out—which really translated to her knowing how to avoid Monica's wrath at all times. So if she was calling Karena at almost ten o'clock on a weeknight then it must be urgent.

"Who is the message from? Maybe I can handle this before Monica returns," Karena said since she had no idea what her sister was doing or when she would return.

"It's from a Yates Hinton. I've never heard the name before and he's not a client. But he's been calling here nonstop. I think the package is from him, as well. He says its imperative that he speak to Monica as soon as possible. He even asked if I could give out her cell-phone number or the number to where she's staying."

Karena was not happy that Adonna had been right. If Adonna hadn't heard of someone and they were calling the gallery for Monica then it couldn't be about gallery business. Which was strange because everyone knew Monica didn't have a personal life.

"Give me his number. I'll give him a call and see what I can get out of him."

While Adonna read off the number Karena motioned

for Sam to get her something to write with. As she jotted down the name and number she assured Adonna she would take care of everything and not to worry. Even though a very small part of her had begun to do just that.

Disconnecting with Adonna, Karena immediately dialed the number she'd written down and received an automated voice-mail message. With a frown she left a message stating that she was calling for Monica and that he could get in touch with Karena instead.

"What was that all about?" Sam asked the moment she finished leaving the message.

"Monica's assistant says this guy's been looking for Monica and sent some package to the gallery for her. He's being very persistent so Adonna wanted to know if I knew when Monica would be back so she could give this man some type of answer."

"Isn't it her job to brush people off until Monica gets back?"

Karena nodded, looking down at the slip of paper she'd written the number on. "Yeah, it is. And Adonna's usually really good at it. So if she's calling me, this guy must really be working her nerves. Anyway, I told him he can contact me if what he needs is urgent."

"But you don't think it is?" Sam asked, watching his wife carefully.

"Truth is, I don't know what to think about it. I've never heard this guy's name before so I wonder how he even knows Monica."

"She's not a hermit, Karena. She's made a lot of business connections. Maybe she's following up on more stock for the gallery."

"Maybe," Karena said, sitting back and vowing to

enjoy the back rub her husband was so intent on giving her. But "maybe" didn't sit well with her.

Monica's eyes closed of their own accord as contentment flowed generously through her body. It started at her feet, right in the center, then up to the balls, over the toes then back down to the heels. Sensations moved from that locale upward, settling in her calves until they were warm and tingling, easing up to her thighs until they had their own heat spearing through them, pressing into her center that now throbbed and wept for attention of its own. Her breasts were heavy, nipples tingling; her arms felt languid, her mouth slack as her tongue slid slowly over puckered lips.

Alex was giving her a foot massage.

But it felt as if he were massaging every part of her body. She'd never felt so relaxed and simultaneously aroused before in her life. He'd taken a few pillows from the sofa, laid them on the floor and instructed her to lie on them. She did as he asked even though she wasn't totally sure she should. When she'd been in the bedroom there was a chill in the air, an attestation to the fact that the electricity was out. Since the cabin obviously operated on all things electric, there was no heat. But here, in front of the still-roaring fire and being touched by this man, Monica was on fire.

She knew she should tell him to stop. Every time he touched her, every time they were together, memories of her past crept closer to the surface. Alex was a different kind of man, she kept telling herself. Still, she'd thought she'd known before, thought the man was exactly who he said he was. She'd been wrong.

When his hands moved from her feet to cup her

calves then up even farther to brush along her thighs, Monica shivered and twisted a little. His touch grew stronger, fingers pressing into her inner thighs. While her heart hammered in her chest, her vaginal muscles clenching with expectation, the increased pressure from his hands changed something in her mind.

Monica tried to move again, wiggled so that she would be free of his grasp. She heard him mumble something but his hands didn't leave her body. He was closer now, his lips brushing along her jawline. She turned her head, but still didn't open her eyes. Pressing her elbows into the pillows and her heels to the floor, she tried to move away, to get away. But he was heavy and he was on top of her, holding her hostage…again.

She had to get away, that was all Monica could think. So she began kicking, her arms flailing, slapping against him. She wanted to scream but no sound came from her mouth. All she knew was that she had to get away, to keep him away. He wasn't going to do this to her, she wouldn't let him, not ever again.

When her palm connected with his cheek, her knee barely missing his groin, Alex knew something had happened. They'd gone from a sensual foot rub to something he couldn't explain. Her eyes were closed so for a second he thought maybe she was asleep. But no, she'd been with him just a minute ago. Moaning and panting, wanting his touch as desperately as he'd wanted to touch her. Then she'd gone buck wild. Instincts had him catching her wrists before she could slap him again. He half rolled off her just to get out of the line of fire of her flailing legs, but he held her wrists. He gave her a shake until her eyes opened. Alex wasn't pleased with what he saw.

"Get away from me! Let me go!" she yelled.

He recognized fear when he saw it and figured the best thing to do was to gain back a level of trust. It was obvious she was mistaking him for someone else but she wasn't up to hearing that right now. So Alex let her go, got to his knees then stood watching as she scrambled across the floor, putting distance between them. When she finally stood he took a step toward her.

"No!" She held out both arms to stop his procession.

"Just take a couple deep breaths," he instructed her from where he stood. "You're not there anymore, baby. You're here with me."

She was shaking her head, her long hair swishing and wrapping around her shoulders like a cloak. "I won't go there again. I won't."

"You don't have to," he said with rage so raw his throat felt scratchy. He wanted to touch her, to wrap his arms around her until she felt safe again. Instead he took one tentative step toward her.

"I can't do this," she whispered, her hands covering her face.

Alex was beside her now, reaching out to touch a hand to her shoulder. "It's okay. Everything's okay now. I won't let him hurt you."

More like he'd kill the sonofabitch if he even thought about putting a hand on her again. Because Alex knew this fear, he knew that look she'd had in her eyes, the fight-or-flight way she'd gotten the hell away from him. That look would be permanently etched in his mind after seeing the way his last secretary looked every morning after her husband had beat her. Every morning except the one when she hadn't come in to work, because the jerk had finally killed her.

Now he was seeing it again and hating it even more because this time it was Monica. Everything in him wanted to fight, to kill, to claim this woman from the man who'd terrorized her—the bastard who'd hit her.

"No," she said without the punch her voice had held before. She took another step away from him and looked up at him, not bothering to fix her hair or stand in that ramrod-straight way she normally did with her chin held high.

What she looked right at this very moment was defeated and still afraid, maybe not of him but of what she'd remembered, what she'd thought might be happening to her again.

"I need to get out of here. I need to go home."

"Baby, listen to me—"

"I'm not your baby," she said defiantly. "I'm nobody's baby."

Alex nodded. "Monica."

"Don't, Alex. I'm not doing this with you. None of this. Let's just forget about the last couple of days, forget we were stranded here. Just forget it all."

"I can't do that" was his honest reply.

"Then that's your problem," she said before turning and running into the bedroom, slamming the door behind her.

He wanted to go after her, wanted to demand she open the door, or, hell, kick the damn thing in. But he didn't.

Instead he went to the couch and sat down, let his head fall into his hands and prayed that he'd never come face-to-face with the bastard stupid enough to put his hands on Monica Lakefield.

Chapter 13

Alex awoke the next morning to a searing pain in his back from sleeping on the couch and a slight chill because the fire had long since burned out. He'd had a blanket but it wasn't conducive to his six-foot-three-inch-and-a-half stature so the bulk of the night he'd spent uncovered. When he sat up, letting his feet fall to the floor, a sound coming from outside startled him.

He went to the window and was partially relieved to see a snowplow making its way down the path in front of the cabin. He went to the first rustic-looking lamp he saw and switched it on. The electricity was back and the plows were out.

Monica would be ready to find her own room.

That thought hit him with a pang. After last night he definitely wanted more time with her. He wanted to know what had happened to her and he wanted to help her cope with her past so she could move on with her future. Even more so, he wanted the guy's name who'd put his hands on her. Alex knew that was a tidbit of information Monica would never willingly give him. Still, he planned to find out anyway.

He found his cell phone in the dining room and dug through one of his bags for the charger. After plugging it into the wall, he waited until the green light signaled it was charging. Then he went back into the living room to find the cell phone that Monica had reluctantly abandoned two days ago. Alex found her charger right next to it and plugged it into the wall. He wasn't certain it would work since when he removed the battery it looked as if the device had sustained substantial water damage. But he'd give it a try, for her. No doubt she'd be looking for the phone the minute she awakened and realized the electricity was back on.

Alex then retrieved his laptop, went back to sit on the couch he'd cursed all night and waited for it to boot up. He wanted to send a couple of emails before dealing with Monica and her stubborn attitude this morning. First, he sent a quick email to Renny to let him know that both he and Monica had braved the storm and were now among the land of the living with electricity and heat. He emailed a quick hello to his parents. Then he opened another email box and began to type.

Monica had been up for hours. To tell the truth, she'd never really fallen asleep. Guilt and embarrassment were worse than caffeine when it came to going to sleep. She'd lain in that bed staring at the ceiling, pulling the blankets up to her neck since she wasn't about to ask Alex to light the fireplace in the bedroom, and she'd closed and locked the door so any semblance of heat from the fireplace in the living room wasn't getting in. That didn't matter; she could survive the cold. Surviving the humiliating scene that had played out in the living room wasn't going to be as easy.

She'd acted like a complete idiot. Well, to her credit, she hadn't been able to help it. The past had mixed with the present and that wasn't good. She remembered the past so vividly even though it had become her daily mantra to forget. The past had been humiliating, as well. The present—Alex—wasn't supposed to end this way. It was going to end. Whatever was going on between them, that was a given. She couldn't have it any other way. But it was supposed to end on her terms, with her walking away head held high. Instead she'd run away, again.

About two hours ago she'd realized the electricity was back on and she'd snuck out of the room to finally get a hot shower and change her clothes. Now her bags were packed and she was more than ready to leave this cabin and find her own room until she could secure a return flight back to New York. She could have left an hour ago, but something about sneaking out while Alex slept didn't sit well with her. She couldn't run forever. Besides, Alex struck her as the type of man who'd show up on her doorstep back home. Better she get the confrontation with him over with now.

It was almost ten in the morning when she put her bags on her arms and walked out of the room. The cabin was quiet and she wondered if Alex was actually still asleep. She'd thought she heard him moving around, but outside her window she'd noted there was some cleanup activity going on. Wherever the noise had come from she was on her way to the living room and then to the door.

Alex was already there.

She stopped the moment she saw him standing near the door. He had on his coat and boots and looked even more delicious than he had when he was dressed only in sweats and a T-shirt. Today, however, he also looked dangerous. When he heard her approach he turned to look at her.

"Mornin'," he said in a deep drawl. His eyes took in everything, from her neatly pulled-back hair to the tips of her black leather boots and no doubt the bags she had draped over her shoulder.

Monica stopped, stood still and said, "Good morning."

"I was just going to check to see if they've finished shoveling the front path. I'm all packed and rented a car already so we can be on our way just as soon as the roads out are cleared."

"We?" she asked, trying to digest everything he'd said.

He'd just opened the door so chilly air swept inside, making her shiver.

"Yes, we. There are still no available rooms here, but there's a small town just down the mountain. We can drive there, get a room for the night then take the flight out on New Year's Eve. I've already secured us two tickets since we missed our previous flights due to the storm."

"Ah, okay," she said, not sure if he was being high-handed and presumptuous or just kindhearted and considerate. "Have you seen my phone?"

Alex slipped his leather jacket on and took a step

outside. "It's in the living room charging. I suggest you try one of our phones. The battery is more stable and we have a patented waterproof coating. If not, then you're definitely going to need a new battery for yours when you get home."

"Thanks," she replied just as he was closing the door.

When she was alone Monica put down her bags and moved into the living room. Her phone was on one of the end tables plugged into a charger. As she lifted it up she could hear his voice telling her she'd need a new one. Closing her eyes with the phone in her hand she heard him last night trying to calm her, to comfort her. And she'd turned him away.

That had been the right move. Protecting herself was a necessity now, not just the habit that everyone thought it was. She couldn't give any part of herself again, couldn't risk the pain and humiliation she'd endured the last time. So what if she was becoming one of the proverbial angry sistahs with attitude. Monica didn't give a damn what people thought about her.

But maybe she did. Maybe that was the real reason she'd kept what happened in South Carolina a secret. She'd never told anyone, not even her sisters what Yates had done to her. And she never would. No one would believe her—that's what he'd told her. And she believed him. Even after all this time, after all the lies that had been uncovered, after the ultimate betrayal, the one thing Yates had said that she truly believed in her heart was that nobody would ever believe her story.

"We're all set," he said from behind, causing Monica to jump.

She cleared her throat. "All right. I'll just get my coat and my bags." Not turning around to face him, she pulled the charger cord from the wall and wrapped it in her hand.

"I'll take your bags to the car. Button up tight. It's really cold out here."

And then he was gone.

His niceness was going to undo her, Monica was certain. Alex wasn't mentioning what happened last night, no doubt giving her the space he figured she needed to deal with it on her own. She had to respect him for that. The fact that he'd gotten up and secured them a way out of this cabin and back to the city was no small feat and one she was very thankful for, even if she hadn't expressed that to him.

When she was secured in the passenger seat of the white SUV Alex had rented and he was in the driver's seat driving slowly down the slope that led from their infamous cabin retreat, Monica spoke quietly.

"Thank you for being so considerate. I really appreciate it."

"You're welcome."

For the next two and a half hours Alex didn't say another word. And strange as it might seem, Monica really wanted him to. She wanted him to talk about his family or ask about hers, talk about his job or hers or the weather, something. This silence was grating on her nerves.

"I'm not all bad, you know," she heard herself saying before she could question why.

"Never said you were" was his simple reply.

"I know people think I'm a bitch. But I'm really not."

"People usually think one-dimensionally. Your personality gives off cold vibes. It stands to reason people would think you're a bitch."

"But I'm not," she replied adamantly.

"I don't usually think like other people." He glanced over at her before looking back at the road. "I knew there was more to you the first time I saw you."

That held her quiet.

"I knew there was more to you, too." She cleared her throat. "I mean, I knew you were going to be difficult."

"Because I'm tenacious." He smiled. "I've heard that before."

"No. Because I knew you saw something else. It's like no matter what face I put on when you were around, you saw through it." She looked out the window, watching the endless stretch of white that was the hills and land beyond the roads. As for the road itself, it was a slushy dirt-brown mush that took away from the otherwise pristine scenery. The scenery that was sterile, aloof, alone. Why that thought stuck like a brick in her chest, Monica had no idea.

"You can't hide forever, Queen. And whatever happened in your past isn't worth you trying to."

"What happened in your past, Alex? Why aren't you happily married to some wonderful woman, giving her all this caring and compassion you seem to have bottled up?"

"I've had some rocky relationships and the reason I'm not happily married is because I haven't found the right woman."

"The perfect woman, you mean. The woman that you give your heart to has to be perfect, right?"

"No. She has to be the woman for me, the woman that I go to sleep thinking about and wake up wanting desperately to see. I don't care if she's successful in business or a waitress depending on her tips to make her monthly bills. I'm not looking on the outside for the woman of my dreams, but on the inside because that's where she truly is."

She sighed. "So poetic. So thought-out. I should have expected nothing less."

"Do you want to argue, Queen? Or do you want to get to know each other better? I can do both. I just need to know which way the conversation is headed."

"I'm not—" she started to say but was cut off by the abrupt swaying of the SUV.

Alex had been watching the rearview mirror as he'd been talking to Monica. There was a smaller black SUV right behind them. The windows were tinted dark so he couldn't see if it was a man or woman driving. He'd noted how close the other vehicle seemed to be tailing them, but figured maybe the other driver wanted to keep close since they were traveling under the speed limit on the slush-packed road with puddles and patches of snow as well as ice. It was rugged terrain that called for cautious driving. So when the other vehicle had suddenly picked up speed Alex knew it wasn't going to be good.

The black SUV had crossed into the other lane, coming up beside them and turning so that the vehicles would collide. Alex, thinking quickly, turned the steering wheel, pulling their vehicle away from the other one. Monica didn't scream but held on to the handle over the passenger window as the SUV jerked and swayed.

They must have hit a patch of ice because suddenly the tires went haywire, the steering wheel becoming only a fixture in the truck as Alex lost all control. Extending an arm outward and over Monica's chest, he attempted to protect her as they tumbled onto the side of the road. A hill of snow blanketed the front half of the truck, planting them lopsided on and off the road.

When their vehicle stopped Alex fumbled to get the seat belt off. "Stay here!" he yelled at Monica then pushed his door open and jumped out into the snow.

How he thought he was going to run after the other vehicle when the snow came up to his knees Alex had no clue, but he stomped through, kicking snow everywhere in his attempt.

The other vehicle sped off, kicking up more snow and slush in a rain of white as Alex's curses joined the commotion.

After making his way back to the truck, he went right to the passenger-side door and reached for the handle. He was shocked to find Monica still holding the handle, her entire body shaking. Clenching his teeth at the sight, he took a deep breath then reached over to undo her seat belt. With careful motions he touched her fingers, unwrapped them from the handle and pulled her into his arms.

"It's okay, Queen. You're okay. Just a little fender bender." He held her close. Alex had a suspicion it was more than that.

Chapter 14

The interior of the truck hadn't reached the freezing point yet. Alex had moved them to the backseat, pulling out blankets that had been stored there by the resort just in case. *A good thing the staff had the sense to think about "just in case,"* Alex thought as he and Monica slid closer on the backseat. He wrapped an arm around her and they both pulled at their ends of the blankets until they were covered up to their chins.

"How long did the tow truck say they'd be?" Monica asked, trying desperately not to shiver again. She was cold and she was more than a little shaken up by the accident, but Alex had already held her and she'd already assured him she was fine. It was time she acted like it.

"About an hour," he said, pulling her even closer.

"So we'll just stay like this, hoping our combined

body heat and these blankets will keep us warm until they get here?"

"Sounds like a plan," he responded with a wry chuckle. "You comfortable?"

She was, surprisingly. With her body tucked against his and the two thick blankets wrapped securely around them, Monica was beginning to feel better. She was beginning to feel safe.

"Yes," she finally responded. "That other driver was a maniac. I can't believe he didn't even stop to see if we were okay. I wish I'd gotten his license number so I could report him."

"Don't worry about it," Alex said. "Let's talk about something else. Something cheerful."

"You want cheerful when we're stuck in this truck that's stuck in the snow?"

He chuckled, but it didn't sound sincere. "Humor me."

Okay, Monica thought. She could do that. Alex had jumped out of the truck and had been moving ever since to get them help and make them as comfortable as possible in these circumstances. If being cheerful was the least Monica could do, she'd certainly give it a try.

"When I was ten I wanted to be a superhero."

The interior of the truck was instantly silent.

Monica took a nervous breath but wouldn't look at Alex. "I used the sheet from my bed and tied it around my neck. I'd been in ballet for two years by then so I had leotards and tights in every color imaginable. I put the blue ones on and pretended my green-and-white floral-print sheet was red and used it for a cape. When my costume was complete with my red leather rider boots I stood on the wrought-iron edge of my full-size canopy bed and jumped.

"The plan was to fly across the room to the dresser. Nothing big, I was just practicing. You know, building my way up to things like flying down the steps, into the den and eventually out the front door up to the sky. So, I misjudged the distance or the floral sheet wasn't as helpful as I thought it should be. Afterward I thought maybe because it was the wrong color. Anyway, I leaped off the bed and was airborne for about ten seconds before the side of my face crashed into the edge of the dresser."

"Ow" was Alex's surprising reply.

Monica only nodded, remembering the pain that came about twenty seconds after the collision.

"At first I was just dazed, but happy that I'd made progress. My dresser was a couple feet away from the bed. Then my mother barged into the room. Karena and Deena, who I had dubbed 'action news' because they reported everything that I did or said to my mother without delay, were right behind her. All three of them just stared at me for a few minutes. Then my mother went into action. She was scooping me up off the floor, yelling for Karena to get towels and for Deena to grab the phone and call 911."

"Were you crying?"

She shook her head. "No. I didn't cry until later that night when we finally made it to the emergency room and the doctor said he'd have to stitch my eye closed. Then, you could have told me Santa Claus was in the next room with a bag of goodies just for me and I wouldn't have shut my mouth."

Alex did laugh then and Monica found herself joining right in. The memory was still so clear in her mind even though she hadn't talked about it in years and she'd never talked about it to someone she wasn't related to.

On impulse she reached for his hand and lifted it until his fingers could brush over the barely there scar embedded now beneath her professionally arched eyebrows.

"My war scar," she told him and was surprised into silence when he leaned over and replaced his fingers with his lips for a tender kiss.

"There. All better."

Monica sighed. "My hero."

Settling back and pulling Monica even closer to him this time, it was Alex's time to share.

"It was Christmas Eve. I was thirteen. Rico and Renny are three and six years younger than me, and they were there. We wanted to get a peek at our presents before everyone woke up. So we faked sleep early, avoiding the ritual of watching Christmas movies in the den with popcorn and hot chocolate. Gabriella and Adriana loved that stuff. Us boys simply endured it for my mother's sake.

"Anyway, it was around three in the morning when we, the three musketeers, crept down the steps. My mother loves all things Christmas so there was always a huge tree in the Bennett house. Half the den was filled with presents and holiday paraphernalia so that it took her the entire month of January to clean it all up.

"There were so many boxes and we just dug in, opening any and everything. Tossing the dolls and baby carriages aside, grinning like crazy over the Legos, Tonka trucks and army men. We were so busy unwrapping gifts we didn't pay any attention to what Bonkers was doing."

"Bonkers?" she asked quizzically.

"Our chocolate-brown Lab who played just as hard and got into as much trouble as the three musketeers did."

Monica nodded. A grin was already spreading across her face. She hadn't pegged Alex for a pet guy, but could clearly hear the love in his voice as he spoke of Bonkers.

"Bonkers wanted to get in on the opening of gifts, as well. So he'd loped on over to the tree, scooting on his stomach until he was firmly beneath it, and grabbed hold of a box. The box probably lodged on a branch or something and Bonkers became frantic with trying to retrieve his catch. It was too late the moment the three of us looked up and Rico whispered for Bonkers to stop. The dog was too far gone, his package firmly between his teeth as he continued the tug-of-war. We'd just stood up to go and get him when it started to tilt."

"What started to tilt?"

"The tree," Alex said with a sense of dread. "All eight-and-a-half feet of Douglas fir tilted and wobbled before falling on top of Bonkers and the three musketeers."

Monica laughed so hard and so fast she didn't have time to think of whether or not it was appropriate.

Their laughter subsided only to be replaced by a sort of needy silence. The closeness could not be denied, not only physically but intimately. Beneath the blankets Monica felt warmth radiating between them. One of his arms was wrapped around her shoulders and the other rested in front of them on his lap. Both her hands were in her lap until he lifted his hand and cupped her chin, titlting her head up to his. She touched his elbow then, rubbing her hand over his biceps and back again.

For an endless moment he simply stared into her eyes. She stared back at him, and though no words were spoken they communicated. He wanted to kiss her. She wanted to kiss him. It wasn't the time; then again, it was. Never again would they be in such a simplistic setting, waiting for one thing and one thing only. The hustle and bustle of her work life and his was not an obstacle here. Their families were thousands of miles away. Right here, right now it was just the two of them.

When his lips brushed over hers Monica sighed in relief. Waiting another moment was going to be damn near impossible for her. If need be, she was prepared to initiate the kiss herself. But that wasn't an issue any longer. His lips moved over hers slowly, his tongue snaking out to touch each corner of her mouth then stroke long, languid lines over her lips. Her next sigh had her lips parting, her own tongue searching for his. Their tongues sought and mingled even without their lips touching. It was a sensual dance, an intimate mating that sent shivers throughout her body.

Monica let herself stay right there, ensconced in his warmth, his protective embrace. She didn't think logically, didn't want to be cautious and didn't for one moment imagine what might lie ahead.

The tow truck showed up two hours later and its surly, overweight, cigar-smoking, short-sleeve-wearing-the-day-after-a-blizzard driver did, too. Alex helped Monica out of the backseat of the SUV. Afterward she stood on the side of a snowy bank watching it being hitched to the back of the tow truck.

"Come on," Alex said, holding a hand out to her. "He's going to give us a ride into town to the nearest hotel."

She nodded but didn't try to talk as she gingerly stepped through the snow to the passenger side of the tow truck. For the next forty minutes she was pressed between big cigar man and Alex, who had wrapped his arm around her shoulders again, pulling her closer to his side than that of the driver's.

When they finally arrived at the gloriously named Room at the End Hotel, which sat just on the edge of a picturesque little snow village, Monica was hungry and sleepy, which translated to cranky. Alex got his first taste of her mood when he'd stepped up to the front desk, gave his name and requested a room.

"And if you have another room I'll take it," she said, giving him a stern look before she turned her attention back to the clerk.

"Two rooms?" the clerk asked, looking at both of them, probably knowing that they'd come together since the tow-truck driver had come in here just before them to use the facilities.

"No."

"Yes."

They answered simultaneously.

The clerk held up a hand when they both were ready to speak again. "I have an adjoining on the fourth floor."

"We'll take it," Alex said immediately, then gave Monica a look that said she should keep quiet.

She also looked as if she was debating whether or

not to go along with him. Eventually—like when the clerk handed both of them keys—she looked resigned to their fate.

Once they were out of the elevator and walking down the hallway to their rooms she said, "I meant what I said about us forgetting about what happened in the cabin."

"And I meant what I said."

She sighed as she came to her door and flipped the credit card–like key between her fingers. "Alex, this just isn't smart for either of us."

"You can tell yourself that all you want, Queen. But each time you kiss me I get a different message."

"Then maybe I should stop kissing you."

He shrugged and put his own key card into the slot on the door. "You could try that but I'm almost positive it won't work."

"Why won't it work?" Alex could hear the puzzlement as well as the apprehension in her tone.

He pushed his door open, then looked over to her. "Because I have no intention of stopping anything where you're concerned."

"No means no," she said snidely and unlocked her door.

"See, that's the problem, Queen. Your nos don't tell me to stop. They allow you to retain some kind of defense in your mind, but your actions speak much louder. But rest assured, the moment you tell me to stop and mean it with your heart, I will."

"And then what?"

"Then you'll be the one coming to me."

She pushed her door open and took a step inside.

"Don't bet on that," she said, letting her door close with a loud clank.

Alex only smiled.

He was wearing her down, he could tell. And that thought almost made him feel better about the jerk who'd just tried to run him off the road. Almost.

Chapter 15

Monica had just stepped out of the shower. Her hair was wet and she was tucking the towel under her arms when she heard a loud thump. Instantly she looked toward the balcony doors. There was a heavy curtain pulled closed over the sheer one and she'd already checked to ensure it was locked before she'd gone into the bathroom. Yet Monica was certain the sound she heard had come from that direction.

There was another thump and she knew she should have moved, probably run out of the room, but that really wasn't her style. Instead, she moved closer to the bed, lifted the lamp and pulled the plug out of the socket. Whoever was on her balcony was going to get an unwelcome surprise the moment they stepped foot into this room. She took a step closer, her legs slightly parted as she grabbed the lamp tighter in her hand, lifting her arms ready to strike.

But instead of the intruder working the lock to get in there was a loud crash and wind whipped into the room, the curtains at the balcony doors lifting behind it. Glass showered the room, catching Monica's bare shoulders and her face. She blinked but tried to remain focused, waiting for whoever it was to come into the room.

Behind her the door to her room was kicked open. Just as she was about to turn to see who intruder number two was, she glimpsed the one from the balcony, dressed in all black with a ski mask over his head. Monica hurled the lamp at his head instead of keeping it in her hand and whacking him with it. He dodged the assault just as she was grabbed by the waist and pulled away.

Without even turning she knew who held her and was furious that he was there. "Put me down!" she screamed as he lifted her off her feet and carried her to the door. "He's getting away!" She pounded her fists on his arms but that was useless. He wasn't letting her go.

"Calm down. I already called the police. He ran out onto the balcony. We're four stories up. By the time he climbs back down either the police or hotel security will be down there," he said when he finally put her down in the narrow corridor of the hallway.

She spun around, wet tassels of hair slapping against her cheek. "What are you, some bodyguard or something? Why'd you come over here? I thought we agreed we needed our space."

"First," Alex said calmly, "lower your voice or all the occupants that didn't hear the window breaking are going to hear you screaming and come out to see what's going on." She started to speak but Alex clapped a hand over her lips to keep her quiet. "Second, I'm in the adjoining room, remember? I heard the noises on the balcony and was coming over to check on you. I started to break through the adjoining door but I was trying to observe the space that you think we need. And third, I'm going to leave you right here for a second, run into that room and get your robe before I have to beat every cop and/or male worker in this hotel to death for looking at you half-dressed as you are."

He waited a beat and lifted his brows as if to ask if she understood what he'd said. Monica nodded reluctantly, hating to give in to him on any level. Then he removed his hand and turned away, ducking into the room where her clothes were. He was back in a couple seconds, clutching her robe in his hands. When she reached for it, he wrapped it around her shoulders.

"Now, when the police get here tell them exactly what happened. We'll let them search the room then get your things. You're staying in my room tonight and I don't want to hear another word about it."

Monica huffed. "Sure, I'll just stand here and speak when you tell me to and shut up when you say so, just like a puppet."

He cut her a glance when she pushed his hands away as he'd been trying to tie her robe around her. "I can do it myself."

"I know you're independent, Queen. But sometimes you just need to sit back and let somebody take care of you for a change."

"I don't need you to take care of me."

"Everybody needs somebody."

Two uniformed police officers stepped off the elevator before Monica could reply, which was probably a good thing because this conversation was starting to border on juvenile for her.

Keeping one arm around her, Alex extended his other hand to both the officers one at a time, introducing himself and her.

"It was your room that was broken in to?" The first officer, the tall lanky one with the fuzzy mustache and the badge that read Cooper, asked.

"Yes," Monica answered before Alex dared to answer for her. Even though she wasn't feeling her best after seeing the man jump through the window, she wasn't a simpering mess, either. She could talk for herself just fine. "I had just come out of the shower when I heard noises on the balcony. I picked something up to defend myself just before the glass shattered and the guy was standing in the middle of the room."

"What'd he look like? Did you know him?" Officer number two was a few inches shorter than Officer Cooper and had a full dark beard and mustache. His badge read Harrington.

"He wore a ski mask," she said then thought how trivial that must have sounded since they were so close to the ski capital of the world. "All black. Kind of short. That's all I remember since it was so quick."

"As soon as I came in he jumped off the balcony," Alex added.

"And where's your room?" Officer Harrington asked.

Monica noted that neither officer had pulled out a notepad. They both just looked from her to Alex with somewhat bored facial expressions.

"We have adjoining rooms. I heard the noise on her balcony, as well, and came over to see if she was okay," Alex said.

"And why wouldn't she be okay?" Officer Cooper asked. "Did you know ahead of time that someone was going to break in to her room?"

Monica stared incredulously at the officer for asking such a ridiculous question. At her side she felt Alex stiffen and wondered if he were about to lose his temper.

Instead he answered in a calm tone, "We had another incident on our way here. Someone tried to run us off the road. So, yes, I was worried about her safety. Hearing the noises alerted me to the fact that something might be wrong."

Officer Harrington cast a glance at Officer Cooper, who nodded his head.

"You two married?" Cooper asked.

What the hell did that have to do with anything?

"No, we're not," Monica answered briskly. "Don't you want to check out the room? Maybe dust for fingerprints?"

"Hold on, little lady," Harrington said, raising a hand in Monica's direction. "We're conducting this investigation."

"Are you really?" Alex said to Harrington. "Look, that's the room the guy broke in to. Did you manage to catch him coming off the balcony?"

"Nah," Cooper answered. "Crowd's pretty thick downstairs in the lobby and outside. With only an hour till the party, people are everywhere."

So that meant they weren't going to catch the guy and weren't even going to try looking for him.

"Fine. I've told you all I know. Can I go now?" Fed up with the jerk officers, Monica shifted from one foot to the other.

"You want to file a written report?" Harrington asked.

"Don't you think she should?" Alex responded.

Cooper hunched his shoulders. "If nothing was stolen and nobody was hurt, might not be worth it."

Or if they were of a different race it would change the circumstances dramatically, Monica thought and could tell Alex was probably thinking the same thing. But instead of calling the race card, they both just stood straighter, looking each officer in the eye.

"She'll stay in my room tonight, and I'll make sure she's safe. We're leaving in the morning so you don't have to worry about taking time from your New Year's celebration to write down a report. But know this," Alex said in a deadly serious tone. "If this guy comes near her again while we're here I'm going straight to your superiors with my complaints about the two of you."

"Now, hold on there, son. We came up here, didn't we? Just doesn't look like there's much to go on. She can't identify anybody and you can't, either, seeing as you got there a mite too late. Doesn't seem to me there's a lot to report except for the window damage."

"And I'm sure the hotel would like that reported for insurance purposes," Monica added.

"If that's all, gentlemen, we'll bid you good-night," Alex said, pulling Monica away before either of the officers could speak again.

"Jerks," Monica mumbled as Alex escorted her to his room.

"Big-time. But don't worry, one call to D&D Investigations and I'll have them both taken care of."

Monica recognized the name of the private investigation firm as the one Sam and Trent Donovan ran. If Alex was planning on calling them those joker officers would be reprimanded by the highest authority in Colorado by morning.

"There's a pre–New Year's Eve party going on downstairs in the ballroom," Alex said when Monica came out of the bathroom, dressed in gray lounge pants and a long gray shirt.

"I'll be fine right here," she replied.

She moved to sit on the edge of the double bed. Since they'd walked in off the street and asked for a room, on a holiday no less, they had to take what was available. He was sitting in one of the guest chairs that along with the small round table served as the only other furniture in the room besides the dresser and television.

He'd been sitting here since they'd talked to the police and retrieved Monica's things from her room. Using his phone he'd returned Renny's email asking when they'd be home and sent another email to Sam Desdune. Something wasn't right and the sooner Alex found out what was going on, the better he was going to feel.

"Are you sure you're okay?" he asked, knowing already what her answer would be.

"You asked me that before I went into the bathroom and I said I was fine."

"I'm asking again because you look a little shaken up."

She shook her head. "Why would I be shaken up? Because some maniac just broke in to my room?"

And because another maniac just tried to run us off the road. Alex didn't say that part aloud. "Anybody would be a little off after such an eventful day, Queen.

You don't have to feel like it makes you any less of a person."

"Stop telling me what to feel or what not to feel. How to act, how not to act. Do you think just because we slept together you can tell me how to live my life? I've been doing just fine all these years."

She'd jumped up off the bed and was now pacing the room as she talked. Her agitation was apparent, unfortunately only to him. For that reason Alex remained quiet. Monica was the type of person who needed to work through her own emotions; she didn't want anyone doing that for her. He could respect that. What he couldn't do was sit idly by and let her suffer. That just wasn't going to happen.

"I'm going to go downstairs, grab something to eat and maybe a drink. I'll bring you something back," he said.

She didn't even turn to him, just mumbled something that sounded like "okay."

The minute the door closed Monica sat on the bed again, sighing heavily.

Something was going on. Whatever Alex Bennett thought she might be, stupid wasn't on the list. What were the odds that someone would try to run them off the road, then a couple hours later, someone tries to break in to her hotel room? No, she wasn't stupid. Whatever was going on definitely involved her and possibly Alex.

Moving from the bed, she picked up her purse and searched for her cell phone. The pack up and drive here had happened so fast she hadn't had a chance to call home. Besides, her phone had taken forever to charge. Alex was right; she was going to have to suck it up and get a new phone. But first, she needed to check in with her office. Monica bypassed to her voice mail and listened to more than fifteen messages and three hangups. It was after nine at night so Adonna wouldn't be there, but she left her assistant a message letting her know she would be home tomorrow afternoon. Alex, forever the hero, had already booked them a flight out first thing in the morning.

Monica berated herself, something she did all too often as of late, for not openly appreciating all that Alex had done for her while they'd been stranded. He could have been a total jackass and simply ignored her, but he hadn't. Even after they'd had sex she was pushing at him and he simply took whatever she dished out in his own way, of course. What the hell was wrong with her?

Any other woman with a half bit of sense would be dying to have a man like Alex Bennett falling for her. But that was just it, Monica didn't believe he was falling for her. Alex was a natural-born fixer. He would try to help anyone he thought was in trouble, and for whatever reason he really believed she had issues that he could resolve. If he'd just listen to her she could tell him that her issues would never be resolved, not by another man anyway.

After punching in a speed-dial number, Monica put the phone to her ear and tried to block out her traitorous thoughts.

"Hi, Karena, it's me," she said in a solemn voice. The less her sisters knew about what was going on with her, the better. Monica had always believed that.

"Hey, Monica!" Karena sounded genuinely happy to hear from her. Monica wondered what her sister had thought Alex Bennett was going to do with her. And if they thought it might be bad, then why set this little get-together up in the first place?

"How are you? Where are you? Bree called and said Renny heard from Alex and he told him that you were leaving the resort together to find another hotel."

"We did and we're at the new hotel." She wanted to add *in separate rooms* but that wasn't true. Besides, it might lead to more questions than she was willing to answer.

"And when are you coming home?"

"Tomorrow" was her quick reply.

"Oh, good."

"Is it?" Monica inquired.

"What's that supposed to mean?"

"I don't know. Is it good that I'm coming home after being tricked to take a trip across the country, then get stuck in a blizzard? Oh, and let me not forget that this was a matchmaking trip orchestrated by my own flesh and blood."

Karena cleared her throat. "We didn't mean any harm."

"What you meant and what happened are two different things," she snapped.

"What happened? Did he do something to you? Are you okay?"

"Really, Karena, if you thought he was capable of doing something to me, why would you set something like this up?"

"Alex Bennett is a nice man, Monica. We just thought the two of you might hit it off."

"And then what? What did you see happening beyond this little tryst?"

"I don't really know. Monica, are you okay?"

"I'm fine," she snapped. "Look, let's just forget this whole thing. I don't want to talk about it anymore. What's done is done."

"You sure he didn't do anything to you?"

Monica inhaled deeply, then exhaled slowly. "How are you and the baby, Karena?"

"We're doing well. Dr. Devaris says everything is going along nicely."

"And how's Deena?"

"She's fine. Her and Max are planning to bring the baby back once the weather breaks here on the East Coast. I loved seeing little Sophia. She has the cutest dimples."

"Yes, she does. Deena's doing a great job as a mother," Monica said and knew the words had taken Karena by surprise because her sister became very quiet. "Nothing's wrong with me, Karena. I just think maybe being a mother is something Deena was meant to do. You'll be great with your child, as well."

"And so will you when you find yourself a husband so you can have one."

"I can have a baby without having a husband, Karena."

"Yeah, try telling that to Mama and keeping all your teeth." Karena chuckled.

"Anyway," Monica said with a small smile. There was some truth to Karena's last statement. Noreen Lakefield wasn't the single-parent type of woman. Although Monica had no doubt her mother would love any grandbaby that came her way. "That's not what I called to talk about. How's everything at the gallery?"

"All good on that front," Karena said. "Adonna's got

things under control and I check in with her periodi-
cally to see if there's anything I need to deal with in
your absence."

"Good. Well, I left Adonna a message that I'll be
back tomorrow but probably won't see her until the day
after since it'll be late on the East Coast when I get in."

"You and Alex sharing a flight?"

"Yes," Monica answered. "I'd like to meet with you
on Wednesday to go over some things and see where
we stand with the Black History Exhibit. February's
right around the corner."

"Sure. I think my schedule's clear. So where's Alex?"

"He went to a New Year's party downstairs."

"Why didn't you go?"

Monica frowned, picking at a piece of lint on her
pants. "What for?"

"Ah, to have some fun for a change."

Yeah, that did sound like a good idea. Years ago she
might have actually enjoyed a New Year's party with a
good-looking man. But that was then. "I'm fine here in
the room. Look, I'll call you tomorrow when I land."

"Okay," Karena replied. "And, Monica?"

"Yes?"

"Go easy on Alex. He didn't know about this, either."

"Please, Alex Bennett is a grown man. What do you
mean, 'go easy on him'?"

"I just know how you can be, that's all. And I'm telling you that he doesn't deserve it. We set him up, too."

"Well, if you thought I was going to treat him so bad
then why'd you set him up? Never mind, don't answer
that," Monica replied, squeezing the bridge of her nose
and hoping for some semblance of relief from the headache she'd been nursing for the better part of two hours

now. "Alex and I are both adults. Whatever happens or doesn't happen between us we'll handle just fine."

"So something did happen?"

Monica didn't miss the intrigued tone of her sister's voice and almost gave in and told her what happened. But she didn't; she'd been keeping things to herself for far too long to turn back now. "Let it go, Karena. I'll see you in a couple of days."

"Fine. But I'm just going to have more questions when we meet."

"As long as they're about business I'll answer them," she replied before disconnecting.

She dropped her phone back into her purse and covered her face with both hands. She was a nutcase; there was no doubt about it. She had a caring family and a man who acted as if he could be so much more important in her life and she was sitting here in a hotel room all alone, her head throbbing from worry over her present circumstances and a past that just didn't know how to stay in its place.

The click of the door closing had her jumping and looking over to the door, alert and ready to react if she needed to.

"I brought you something to eat," Alex said, coming closer to where she sat.

"Thanks," Monica said, managing a smile even though it was the last thing she felt like doing. "Look, Alex, I want to apologize—"

"Eat first," he interrupted. "Apologize for making me go to a New Year's party stag, later."

Her smile looked genuine this time and Alex felt the tightness in his gut uncurl. She'd looked so defeated and stressed when he left the room before and he'd hated it.

He wanted the old Monica back, if that was believable. This tired and reserved-looking woman wasn't what he wanted to see.

"How was the party?" she asked as she uncovered the plate he'd brought her. He wasn't totally sure what she liked to eat but he knew she needed to eat something to get that dull look out of her eyes.

"Nothing spectacular. I only went for the food anyway. I brought this for us to bring in the New Year later." He lifted the bottle of champagne he'd stuffed in his front pocket. The back pockets held champagne glasses.

She was biting into one of the salad wraps he'd brought her, the green one. He made a mental note that she obviously liked spinach.

"That'll be nice," she said when she'd finished chewing.

"And then we can talk about what's been going on," he said, not looking at her but putting the glasses and the bottle onto the table and moving to make sure he put the bolt on the door.

"You don't think today's two incidents are coincidence?" she asked.

"No. I don't."

She finished another bite then said, "I don't, either. But I don't have an explanation for them."

"Any enemies? Old boyfriends that want you back?" The last question had been going back and forth in his mind all day. He'd only now figured out how to slip it in.

She picked up the napkin, wiped at her mouth and her fingers. "I had a boyfriend in college. We broke up. I haven't had one since."

Three simple sentences, Alex thought, and he'd touched on what he thought was Monica's biggest problem. Whatever happened in college had clearly dictated how she would conduct the rest of her life.

"Have you seen or heard from him since then?"

"I don't think it's an old boyfriend. He couldn't care less what I'm doing now." After finishing off a mysterious-looking eggroll, Monica picked up the empty plate and took it to the trash can near the door. "Maybe it's a disgruntled client. We both would have those, right?"

"You're right," Alex agreed, but still thought it had something to do with Monica. It had been her balcony the intruder had been on, her window he'd broken. A couple of bucks to the front-desk clerk and it would have been easy enough to find out which room she was in. That's why he'd contacted Sam again.

"Either of us could have been the target," he said to make her feel better. He went to recheck the balcony door, closing the curtains tightly. "Let's not think about it any more tonight. It's New Year's, after all."

She nodded and sat back in the chair at the small table. "That's right. New Year's Eve in a hotel outside of Aspen, Colorado. What better way to ring in the New Year?"

"I'm trying not to take that as an insult." Alex sat on the bed and looked at her.

"No," she said with a sigh. "I'm not insulting you and I'm not trying to be cold or disconnected. It's just—"

"It's just that you don't know how to be any other way," he finished for her.

With a tilt to her head she stared at him. "How do you do that? Every time I say something you can finish it. You know what's in my head before I do, it seems. I've never met anyone like you before, Alex Bennett."

"I believe you," he replied. "Come here." Alex patted the bed beside him and was a little surprised when she didn't hesitate but moved from her chair to come sit beside him. "You don't have to be anybody but yourself when you're with me, Queen. I'm not intimidated by your personality because I know it's just a protective barrier."

"Protection is so much better than defeat, Alex. You're used to protecting your family so I guess you would see that in me."

"What I don't like to see in you," he said, touching a hand to her cheek, "is defeat, for any reason. You're a strong black woman, with a loving family and a successful career. Nobody can defeat you. There should be nobody in your life that you fear, and you shouldn't have to be on guard all the time. I want to take all of that away from you."

"You want the impossible."

"Right now, Queen, I'll settle for just wanting you."

She smiled. "And I'll settle for just wanting you, too."

Moments later they both lay on the pillows at the top of the bed, stretched out on their backs in the dark. It was probably close to midnight, Monica thought, because she could hear people outside laughing and carrying on. There was noise throughout the hallway, as well, as it seemed everyone in the hotel was in a festive mood except for her and Alex.

She liked their mood, too, the quiet contemplativeness of the two of them just lying here alone. His

breathing was slow, measured; she listened and felt
lulled by the sound. Her mind wasn't as full of thoughts
as it had been just a half hour ago. Sure, there were
things going on, but right here at this moment they
didn't seem all that important.

"I've been dating since I was about seventeen,"
Alex's deep voice spoke through the silence. "Over the
years I've been partial to intelligent women, sexy, viva-
cious, good with boundaries."

"Boundaries?" she asked.

"They knew from the start that I wasn't looking for
a commitment and it was okay with them because most
of the time they weren't looking for one, either."

"Convenient." Monica didn't know how she felt
about discussing Alex's past love life. Then again,
they'd discussed hers to an extent. So if he could do it,
she could, too. "I didn't really peg you for the 'love 'em
and leave 'em' type."

"Definitely not. When I walk away it's clear that I'm
doing so. And most of the time it's mutual, so no harm,
no foul."

"I see."

She felt his fingers on hers, let them lace together
and hold tight, forming a bond she wasn't quite sure
what to do with.

"I say all this to let you know that I can't see myself
walking away from you, Queen."

Monica swallowed and wondered if she should say
something. And if so, what?

Alex turned on his side and with his free hand
touched her chin, turning her face to his. "I don't want
to walk away from you."

She didn't have to respond, didn't have a moment to

even consider a response because his lips were already on hers. This kiss was different from all the others they'd shared these past days. It was softer, touching, soothing, coaxing. It was commanding, like confirmation or an announcement. It was deliciously naughty as his tongue slid sensuously over hers.

Of their own volition her arms lifted, wrapping around his strong shoulders, pulling him closer to her. With his other hand now free Alex touched her hip, twined his arm around her and moaned deeper into the kiss.

He pulled her closer, until their bodies were completely touching. Monica pressed herself even closer. She wanted to feel all of him at once. Her body ached with wanting this man and showed its persistence with hips undulating against his, breasts pressing into his chest, arms holding him close.

There was an urgency in the air but the kiss remained slow and seductive. His hands moved up and down her body, gripping her bottom, fanning and rubbing persistently against her back. She mimicked the actions, cupping his bottom in her hands and pressing her now-aching center firmly into his bulging erection.

Alex groaned with that motion and his hands moved under her shirt to find her bare breasts. His fingers toyed with a nipple while his tongue made the same swiping motions over her lips. Monica's breathing was hitched; her eyes closed to the blissful pleasure of his touch. Reluctantly one of her hands left his buttocks to come forward, finding the buckle of his pants and undoing it. The zipper was next, then she was diving inside in search of the erection she craved so desperately. His length was hot and hard in her hand and she stroked him from the base to the tip.

He did the same, letting his hand fan down over her rib cage, to her belly, even farther beneath the elastic band of her lounge pants to her waiting heat. When his fingers first feathered between her swollen lips Monica sighed. He touched her clitoris and her legs began to shake. Stroking slowly, his fingers moved along her slickened folds until finding her aching center and plunging deep.

Monica had no idea how many fingers he used. All she knew for certain was that she felt full, complete, then hungry. She stroked his erection harder, letting her fingertips linger on his moistened tip. Alex pulled his fingers out, plunged in deeper, harder. She lifted one leg, granting him better access. He cursed, swore between their heated kisses, something about wanting to get inside her, needing to feel a part of her.

"Yes" was all Monica could manage to reply and hoped he knew she was responding to everything he'd murmured.

With slow, almost torturous motions he removed her clothes. When she lay there naked and needy he stripped off his clothes, taking his sweet time with each piece. Her vision glazed with lust, Monica watched as Alex lifted his shirt over his head; delectable pectoral muscles and tight abs came into view and her breathing quickened. Perfect buttocks and sculpted thighs appeared next, his thick erection stealing the last of her breath. Her tongue snaked out to lick lips that had gone instantly dry.

He was beyond gorgeous and he wanted her. She

lifted her arms to him, spread her legs slightly and whispered his name.

Alex touched his palms to her thighs; he needed to feel their softness once more. Her skin was shades lighter than his, like freshly churned butter, and his mouth watered each time he saw her naked. She'd parted her legs for him but he wanted more. He wanted to see her, all of her. Reaching over he turned on the lamp and waited to see if she would protest. But she didn't, only watched him with the same hunger he suspected she saw in him.

Again he touched her legs, moved his hands up and down the length, remembering the first time he'd seen them and knew he'd wanted them wrapped tightly around him. Holding both her ankles, he spread her legs wider, his gaze moving swiftly to her center. Like a flower blossoming only for him. Alex's entire body tensed, his hands shaking slightly as they moved upward to touch her there.

Her dewy folds glistened beneath his perusal and his fingertips touched the plumpness lightly. She sighed and he inhaled deeply, exhaling slowly as he lowered his head and kissed her clitoris with a soft peck. He continued to rain kisses over her center, along the soft crevices, near her weeping entrance and back to her clitoris again. Over and over he kissed her, swearing if he never remembered anything else in this world it would be kissing Monica Lakefield this way.

When he felt her hands cupping his head, applying a gentle pressure, he moaned and mumbled a ragged, "Yes." She wanted more and he wanted to give her more. He wanted to give her the world, the sun, the stars, the moon, any and everything he could to make her happy.

Tonight he would give her himself.

Every touch of his lips to her was gentle and filled with everything Alex had felt building inside him for this woman. Since the first day he'd met her he'd known there was something about her, something that had drawn him. She wasn't an easy woman, that was a given, but the man that claimed her would be receiving such a magnificent gift. He wondered if she knew that, wanted her to feel what he was offering wholeheartedly.

His palms gripped her buttocks and he lifted her slightly off the bed, giving himself better access. The sound of her heavy breathing and his name on her lips was like a litany in the air. His arousal was so thick and so hard now it was almost painful. The mere thought of sliding his length inside her was like a touch of heaven.

When she shivered beneath him, her thighs tightening then releasing, her body going limp, Alex lifted his head, dropping a trail of heated kisses over her navel, up her torso to her breasts. She wrapped her arms around his neck as he found her lips and kissed her deeply. Her legs wrapped around his waist and he slipped inside of her without further preamble.

Moving slowly, Alex enjoyed the smooth rhythm they created, the tight friction of her walls gripping his length. There was no need to rush; they had all night. Downstairs there was a party going on—in here it was something else, something special.

Monica couldn't breathe; she couldn't think; she couldn't do anything but feel. Everywhere Alex touched, either with his lips, his hands, his length, everywhere was in the midst of a slow burn.

He'd brought her to release too many times to count, until she felt the way he was stroking inside her now was the grandest of all finales.

Sex had never been this way for her. In the beginning it was exciting, then it was just there, a chore or deed that had to be done, but nothing to this magnitude. She felt something when she was with Alex, something that she'd never experienced before. She couldn't put a name to it, didn't dare to, but recognized its importance just the same.

He'd shifted them so that they were now on their sides, her legs still wrapped tightly around him, one of his hands in her hair, the other splayed securely at her back. He rocked back and forth inside her, keeping their connection and building a slight friction that made her want to scream. It was slow, this lovemaking session, not rushed or fevered like their previous ones. This time was different, Monica knew without a doubt. It was lovemaking this time and not sex.

That thought had her eyes opening.

Alex's were open, too, watching her. His gaze seemed to worship her, to pull her in as if she were the only thing in this room. It was gentle and yet intense. Impulsively she used a finger to trace the outline of his lips, the line of his jaw, his eyebrows, down his nose. She wanted to familiarize herself with every part of him, to dedicate this exact moment to memory in case it never happened again.

"You're beautiful," she whispered.

"So are you" was his reply.

"You see me differently than anyone ever has."

"I see the real you."

His words sounded sweet. They washed over her, coating the intense pleasure he was already giving her. Her eyes fluttered closed as she clung to them, to him.

When he lifted one of her legs, holding it high, and plunged deeper, harder into her, Monica gasped.

"You are my queen," he whispered as he thrust. "All mine, Queen. All mine."

"Yes," she managed to chant over and over again. "All yours."

It wasn't a defeat, she thought as his heated thrusts grew faster, her own pleasure rising higher and higher.

She wasn't giving in, wasn't sacrificing herself. She was accepting, wanting, believing.

And as they reached their release together, Monica realized she was also running. Even as he let her leg slide against his thigh and dropped a parade of kisses along her shoulder, up her neck, on her lips. She was taking all that Alex Bennett had to give and she was running with it, probably away from it. Because she didn't know how to do anything else.

Chapter 16

"I don't want her hurt." Yates sighed with exasperation. "I thought I'd made that perfectly clear."

"You said you didn't like that she was in the mountains with another man and you wanted me to bring her back. That's what I tried to do."

"By almost running her off the road, then breaking into her hotel room? That doesn't sound like what I told you to do." The other man started to speak but Yates waved his words away and interrupted. "She's returning tonight. She'll probably get my package tomorrow, then she'll call me." He looked out the window as he spoke. He was still in New York, still in this crowded and dirty city when he really wanted to be home going about his business. But Monica had broken the rules; she'd done what he'd specifically told her not to do. She should know better. She should know that eventually she'd have to pay for her disobedience.

"I'm booked on the same flight she is," he said as if that made up for the debacle he'd already caused.

Glaring at the phone with growing impatience, Yates sighed again. "No. Just get back here and tail her to her place. If he stays with her, you call me immediately."

"Gotcha. I could just take care of him for you. For a small fee, of course."

"No. Do what I've already paid you for and that's it," Yates said adamantly. Good help was so very hard to find, or, in this case, buy.

Telling Alex she didn't need him to ride all the way to her apartment with her crossed Monica's mind as they waited at the curb after grabbing their bags at the airport. But once she slid into the back and looked out at the familiar scenery a slight unrest settled over her and she began silently thanking him for being there. Although she couldn't quite put her finger on what was bothering her Monica knew that something wasn't right.

Alex told the cabdriver to wait as he helped her out of the car and retrieved her bags from the trunk.

"Lead the way," he said with his now-familiar smile.

She went through the glass doors, speaking to Miguel, the doorman, then heading straight to the elevators. Her mail could wait until morning, she decided as suddenly her body felt beyond tired. Everything seemed to be lagging. Try as she might, her steps even seemed slower than normal as they stepped off the elevator on the eighth floor and moved toward the end of the hall.

She lifted a hand to put her key into the lock then

stopped. Knowing his gaze would be on her, she looked at Alex.

"You okay, Queen?" he asked.

She blinked then took a deep breath. Why she was acting so strange, Monica had no idea. But with a shake of her head she unlocked the door and stepped inside.

"Thank you," she said, motioning for him to put her bags down just inside the doorway.

Alex did just that, then stepped inside and pushed the door closed behind him.

"You look a little off. Are you sure you're going to be all right staying here alone? I can stay if you want."

She shook her head quickly before her mind changed and she said something that would continue the unthinkable between them. He was rubbing his hands up and down her arms as he spoke. Telling him to go became one of the hardest things she'd ever had to do.

But she did it.

"No. I'm fine. You can leave. I know you have a lot to do to get ready for your big meetings next week."

On the plane they'd talked about business, which was a first for them since they'd been together. But it was senseless to keep avoiding a subject that both of them shared a huge interest in. Alex told her about their newest venture in the cell-phone arena and Monica had to admit she was excited for them. She would be one of the first to buy the new phone when it hit the market next week. Likewise, she'd told him about their upcoming exhibits and how they were looking at opening galleries in Miami and Atlanta later this year. It felt really good to be able to talk to someone about her work and have them look as interested in her business as she was in theirs. Just another reason why she should make a clean break from him—and another reason why she hesitated doing so.

"You're more important to me than work, Queen. If you're not comfortable I want to be here for you."

In an attempt to keep things light she lifted the cell phone she'd stuffed into her pocket. "You're only a phone call away," she said with a smile.

"At home I'm about an hour and ten minutes away. If I stay here—"

She put a hand on his chest. With the other she put a finger to his lips. "Shhh. I'm fine. You can go and everything will go back to normal. You'll see."

Alex kissed her fingertips and Monica pulled her hand away from his lips, chastising herself for doing it in the first place.

"By everything you're trying to tell me, *we'll* go back to normal, as well."

She inhaled deeply and let it out with a flurry of words. "I think it's for the best. We're from two different worlds. We don't even live in the same city, and you know the probability of long-distance relationships working."

"You're not normally an excuse maker, which tells me the thought of us being together still makes you uncomfortable."

"It makes me uncertain," she blurted out, then bit her bottom lip to keep anything else revealing from escaping. "Look, Alex," she said finally. "You don't understand. My life is hectic, to say the very least. Yours is busy, as well. Now is just not a good time."

"You can stop at any time, Queen. None of your arguments are convincing me."

Monica sighed and walked away from him. "I'm just

not ready for this," she admitted with her back to him. "I haven't thought about being in a relationship in a long time and in three days I've been intimately involved with you and thinking thoughts that I shouldn't be thinking. It's just not how I work."

"Because you didn't plan it? Because it wasn't on your agenda? You of all people should know that you can't plan every aspect of your life. And that's what makes it worth living. The unexpected, the surprises that bring you more joy than you could ever contemplate having."

Monica remained quiet, looking out the window at the darkening night sky. "The meter's still ticking in your cab."

When his hands touched her shoulders she jumped because she hadn't heard him come up behind her. She thought he was still standing in the doorway.

"Until you tell me no and mean it with your heart I'm going to keep trying." Turning her to face him, he kissed her forehead lightly, touched his lips to her eyelids, the tip of her nose, then finally her lips. "If you can't sleep tonight remember you said I'm just a phone call away."

A soft smile touched her lips as she nodded her agreement.

"Good night, Queen."

"Good night, Alex."

Alone in her apartment, Monica unpacked her bags and was about to head into her bathroom for a shower when she noticed a small box on the nightstand by her bed.

She hadn't had a chance to shop in Aspen and all

the Christmas gifts she'd given or received had been opened already. So the box wrapped in gold paper with a huge red bow on top was a new arrival.

"Open the damn box, Monica, and stop being childish." Chastising herself was something Monica was used to doing. Tonight it seemed unnecessary as a part of her thought she had every right to be a little jittery. Ignoring that part, she reached for the box and forced herself to rip it open quickly.

With the wrappings tossed on her bed Monica tore into the box then stopped cold as she saw the contents.

Staring up at her were glass blue eyes that looked all too realistic. The eyes were a bright contrast to the pure white of the fur. When she had swallowed once, then twice, she finally had the courage to pull it out.

It was a stuffed rabbit.

Similar to one she'd received before. A long time ago.

There was only one person who would give her this again. The only person who'd ever called her Bunny.

"Yates." His name was a whisper on her lips and a pounding to her heart.

Chapter 17

"So give us all the gory details," Renny said, propping his feet up on the edge of the glass-and-marble coffee table in Alex's living room.

Alex wasn't surprised that both his brothers and his brother-in-law were in his apartment waiting for him. He'd told them all the time his flight was coming in but only Sam knew about the two incidents that had occurred in Aspen. Both of his brothers had keys to his place, just as he had keys to theirs. After the incident where the entire Bennett family was stalked and attempts on Renny's and his wife's life were made a couple years back, they all exchanged keys for safety reasons.

"A gentleman never kisses and tells," Alex said, dropping his bags near the bar and reaching for a glass to fix himself something to drink.

Rico laughed. "That's why we're asking you."

Alex returned his brother's grin. They knew him very well, both his brothers—Renny, the tallest of the three Bennett men with his close-cut curly hair and seductive eyes, and Rico with his slanted eyes, thick hair and football-player build.

"It's good to see you made it through the stay in Aspen without a scratch," Sam, the most sober of the group, said with a small smile.

"Who says he doesn't have scratches? They may be carefully hidden," Renny joked.

Meanwhile, amid all the banter, Alex fixed himself a rum and coke and took his first swallow. When the cool liquid coated his throat and he didn't feel as if he was about to jump in a cab and return to Monica's house, he finally spoke. "We had an enjoyable time despite your sorry attempts at matchmaking."

"So there was no match made?" Renny asked.

"You forget I'd already met Monica, long before your little setup scheme. Which, by the way, I want to know, who came up with the idea in the first place?"

Each male stared at each other then back at Alex with fake clueless looks.

"Right," Alex said with a nod. "It must have been the womenfolk, Bree and Gabriella, right?"

Rico chuckled. "Partially. His wife was in on it, too." He pointed at Sam, who simply shrugged.

"The other two Lakefield sisters thought it was an excellent idea," Sam said.

"I'll just bet they did," Alex mumbled, taking another sip from his glass. "For the record, neither Monica nor I thought it was a good idea. We're adults. If we wanted to hook up we would have."

"Yeah, in about six or seven months at the rate you two were going," Rico interjected. "All we did was speed up the inevitable."

"So is she really as bad as she seems?" Renny asked, only to receive wan looks from both Alex and Sam.

"What?" he asked, shrugging his shoulders. "That woman can be a real bitch."

Sam grimaced. "She's my sister-in-law, man. Show some respect."

"And she's not a bitch. So I'll ask you to show me some respect, as well."

All eyes fell on Alex after he said that.

"Thanks to you guys I had the opportunity to get to know her a little better and she's not as bad as she makes people believe she is."

"I don't understand. Why go through the trouble of making people not like you?" This was Rico, who had always asked a lot of questions since his childhood years.

"That's what I want to pick Sam's brain about," Alex said as he walked around the bar to sit on one of the leather chairs in his living room.

"Yeah, I've been thinking about what you said in the email. So a car tried to run you off the road then somebody broke in to Monica's room at the hotel. I don't think the incidents are coincidences."

Alex nodded. "I don't, either. And when she finally calmed down enough to talk about it, Monica agreed with me. She thinks it could be either of us being targeted for our job or social connections."

Sam chuckled. "That sounds just like something Monica would say."

"Wait a minute, somebody want to clue us in to

what's going on? Somebody tried to run you off the road, Alex? When?" Renny asked, concern lacing his voice.

"When we were driving from the cabin into the small town where the hotel was located. Then, after we checked into the hotel, someone broke the balcony doors to Monica's room."

"You're kidding," Rico exclaimed. "Did you call the cops? File a report?"

"Yeah, at the hotel the cops came, asked a couple of questions then went down to the New Year's party. They weren't overly concerned, just thought it was some partygoer already drunk and celebrating."

"Guess they didn't catch him, then?" Sam asked.

"No. He disappeared into the cloud of folks getting ready for the party."

"Convenient," Renny replied. "You think somebody's after her?"

That was exactly what Alex didn't want to think. "I don't know."

"It sounds like it to me," Sam confirmed. "But who would have known she was there?"

"Maybe her assistant told someone," Alex offered but Sam was already shaking his head.

"Negative. She called Karena the other night asking where Monica was and when she would be back. Apparently Monica didn't have time to even tell her assistant where she was going."

"So what did her assistant want Karena to do?" Rico asked.

"She wanted Karena to call this guy because he'd been calling persistently for Monica and sent her some kind of package."

"That sounds like your guy right there," Renny said. "He's calling her and sending her gifts. An old boyfriend maybe?"

Alex sighed. "I asked her that and she told me no. Her old boyfriend wouldn't want her back."

"She's probably right about that," Rico quipped.

"Hey," Alex warned. "That's enough."

Rico looked at Sam, who only shook his head.

"I'll get the name and number from Karena tonight and look into it first thing tomorrow. Where's Monica now?"

"I dropped her off at her apartment," Alex replied.

Rico sat up in his chair. "Alone? You just left her there?"

Alex frowned. "Make up your mind—either you like her or you don't."

"I don't like you leaving a woman who might be a target alone," Rico argued.

"Then that makes two of us. I didn't want to leave her, either. But she insists she's all right."

"Her building's pretty secure," Sam added. "But just in case I'll call and see if I can get someone to keep an eye on her until she gets to work tomorrow."

"I'd appreciate that," Alex said. He'd appreciate that a lot. He'd also appreciate finding out who this man was who was so adamant about getting in touch with Monica. It didn't matter how much she protested, his protective instincts where she was concerned had already kicked into overdrive.

"Hello?" Karena answered her house phone at a little before midnight. Sam was still out, no doubt having a rollicking good time welcoming Alex back home. She'd thought about going to see Monica but figured she'd see her at work tomorrow at their meeting.

"Karena." Monica's voice sounded weak, distressed. Definitely not the normal Monica.

"What's the matter?" Karena asked, instantly thinking of their parents or Deena.

"I ne— Can you come—" She sighed. "Something's happened."

"I'll be right there," Karena said, hanging up the phone and heading to her closet to grab some clothes.

Less than the normal hour it took for Karena to drive from her house in Connecticut to Monica's apartment in Manhattan, she was entering the glass doors, waving at Miguel and heading straight toward the elevators.

Monica definitely did not sound right on the phone and Karena was getting bad vibes the closer she came to her sister.

Karena rang the doorbell, because Monica hated when people knocked on her door instead, and waited impatiently for her to answer. When she did, Karena's heart sank.

"What is it, Monica?" she asked as she stepped inside and closed the door behind her.

Monica simply pointed and Karena followed her gaze toward the bedroom. She started back there, looking to see Monica following her as if in a trance. When she arrived in the bedroom she saw wrapping paper thrown over the bed, a tipped-over box and a stuffed rabbit.

"I don't understand," she said, turning to Monica. "What happened? Did somebody call you and upset you? Was it Alex?"

Monica shook her head and took a deep breath. "It's Yates. He wants me back."

"Who the hell is Yates and what do you mean he wants you back? Let's just sit down and talk about this," Karena said, moving to the bed and pushing the rabbit aside so she could sit down.

Monica sat on the floor right where she'd been standing. She used both hands to run fingers through her hair and reached for the sanity she knew she possessed somewhere.

"Yates and I met when I was a sophomore in college. He was an English professor. Not mine," she said with a nervous chuckle. "That would have been way too cliché."

"Go on," Karena prodded.

"He was handsome and worldly and everything I thought I wanted in a man. He had a great position and he was moving up to the board of directors and making a name for himself in the community. He had political aspirations but wanted to first make his mark in education. When he first approached me I was in awe. Maybe it was because he was twenty years older than me, a man compared to all the boys at school, or it could have been how tall and completely good-looking he was. Whatever the reason, I should have known better.

"But I was only nineteen. Thinking about meeting a mature man while I was away at college wasn't really tops on my agenda. But there he was and he wanted me." Monica shrugged.

Karena watched her closely. "What happened next?"

"He took me to dinner. French restaurants, Italian ones. We had champagne and fine wine and foods I could barely pronounce the names of. That's when Yates suggested I take all the foreign-language classes, especially since I was going for a business degree. He was very well educated so I didn't hesitate to change my schedule. It was perfect. He was perfect. And so I gave him my virginity."

Karena sighed.

When Monica looked up at her she had tears in her eyes and Karena slipped off the bed to sit beside her sister on the floor. She took one of her hands, held it and remained quiet, letting Monica tell the story.

"I gave him everything I had, Karena. Everything. He was my entire world and then he…he let me down."

"How'd he do that?"

Monica cleared her throat. "He was married to some woman from a rich family or something like that. When she found out about us she called me to their house. I'd never been there, not in the three years Yates and I were together. He always took me to a hotel, which, silly me, thought was so very classy. Anyway, his wife wasn't real happy with me, but she wasn't surprised, either, said Yates always picked them young and pretty."

"Oh, honey, I'm so sorry," Karena said, pulling Monica close for a hug. Deena had said something happened to Monica when she was away at school. She'd come home acting distant and had only grown more cynical and judgmental in the years that followed. "He was an ass."

Monica choked out a laugh as she pulled away. "That's an understatement. Anyway, he wanted to continue the affair. I said no. He didn't like that answer and things got ugly for a minute."

"By 'ugly' do you mean *physical?*"

Monica read the alarm in Karena's voice and knew without a doubt Karena would tell her parents and Deena everything she knew. So even though she was telling her this much there were some things, some parts of what turned Monica Lakefield from a young, naive girl into an independent, self-preserving woman, that would remain a secret.

"I mean it wasn't an amicable separation. At one point he made some foolish threat that he'd never see me alive with another man." Monica was shaking her head. "I haven't been with anyone so I don't really know why he's surfacing now. But I know it's him. He used to call me his little bunny. Only Yates would send me that," she said, pointing to the rabbit on the bed.

"Wait a minute. Did you say his name is Yates? Yates Hinton?"

Monica looked alarmed. "How do you know him?"

"He's been calling your office nonstop. Adonna gave me his number to see if I could help him with something. We thought it was gallery business."

Monica shook her head. "No. It's personal. The singularly biggest mistake I've made in my life."

"No. The biggest mistake you made is not telling us about this when you came home. Monica, we're family. You should have known you could trust us. If not Mom and Dad, at least me and Deena. We knew something had happened to you, but you were so closed off about it. I just wish you would have opened up sooner."

"I know. I apologize for that. Keeping the secret has been hard on me, too. Living the life I've had to live, protecting myself from ever getting mixed up like that again, it's all been really tough."

"So you said his threat was if you ever saw another

man, which you made sure not to do all these years. Why's he back, then?"

They both looked at each other.

"I'm not 'with' Alex. This week was just a fluke. Yates couldn't have known about that," Monica started to say then remembered almost being run off the road and the break-in at the hotel. "Oh, my God," she whispered, putting a hand to her chest.

"What? He knew, didn't he? He knew about you and Alex. But how?"

"I don't know. I don't know. It's only been three days, three freakin' days. How did he find out that quick?"

"Actually, it may have been before that," Karena said. "There were pictures all over the tabloids at Deena and Max's wedding. You and I were in the wedding along with Alex. There must have been a shot of the two of you together."

"But that didn't mean we were a couple. Damn, it was just a picture."

Karena looked skeptical. "Yeah, but I remember how the two of you looked that night. When I saw you talking alone I could tell there was something going on between you. We all could. That's why we thought it would be a good idea to set you up in Aspen. It was clear that you were attracted to each other."

She wanted to deny it. Oh, how desperately did Monica want to deny there was something between her and Alex even back then. But it was futile and denial was fast becoming too big a part of her life.

"Dammit!" she yelled and stood from the floor. "After all these years of being by myself, of not letting any man near me for whatever reason, he's been watching all along. Waiting for me to move on, hating that I might actually get over him. Dammit!"

"Don't do this, Monica. Don't let him win. You are entitled to a life without his lying, cheating ass. To hell with him! We'll have him arrested for stalking and harassment and see how he likes sitting in a cell for a while."

Monica shook her head. "No. The news would get out—it would spread. We're trying to expand the gallery, Karena. The last thing we need is bad press."

"Are you serious? You really think the gallery is more important than you standing up to this idiot? Monica, think about what you're saying."

"I know exactly what I'm saying. I'll contact him. We'll talk and this will be put to rest, finally. But I don't want this getting out. I don't want Mom and Dad to know and I definitely don't want it in the papers."

"How do you plan on doing this, then? Maybe we should ask Sam for help?"

"No! The less people that know about this the better. I know you'll tell Deena and that's fine. But nobody else. Promise me, Karena, that you won't tell anybody else about this."

Karena was more than reluctant. She wanted to run home and tell Sam so he could do his investigator thing and find this Yates Hinton. Then she wanted Sam to tell Bree's brother so Cole could use his badge to have the bastard arrested. Then, and this was the best part, she wanted to see the guy herself so she could slug him just once for hurting her sister all these years.

But looking at Monica, for once in her life a vulnerable and frightened woman, Karena couldn't do it.

She couldn't contribute to her sister's heartache. It just wasn't going to happen.

"Fine. I'll keep my mouth shut." After Monica breathed a sigh of relief she added, "But if this gets out of hand, Monica, I'm telling Sam and Mom and Dad. I won't let you be hurt again. Understand?"

"Don't worry. It won't get out of hand. I'm going to deal with Yates Hinton once and for all."

Chapter 18

"Bad news," Sam said the moment Alex answered his phone. "Yates is in New York. His credit card was just used at a hotel in midtown Manhattan." Karena had given Sam Yates's name when they texted earlier.

Alex cursed, slamming his palm on the steering wheel. "Has he tried to contact Monica?"

"I think so. Karena got a call from Monica late last night. She hurried over to her apartment and spent the night. When Karena called me last night she only said Monica wanted some company, which we all know is not like Monica. I've talked to Karena a couple of times today but she hasn't said anything about Monica except that she's fine and in the office. Now, my thought is either Monica had a message from Yates when she got home or he called after you left. Either way it's not good news."

"No, that's not good news. Listen, I've got a meeting with the distribution guys in about twenty minutes. Do me a favor and keep that tail on Monica until I can get into the city."

"Done," Sam said with a nod. "You know she's going to bust your ass for interfering."

"She's going to learn that I'm tougher than her words and chilly looks. I'll call you as soon as my meeting's over for an update."

"No problem."

Sam disconnected the line and rubbed a hand over his stubbly chin. There was a big problem, one Alex hadn't mentioned either time Sam had spoken to him in the past two days.

The matchmaking had proved effective, at least on one person's behalf. He'd known the Bennetts for a while now and if there was one thing he was absolutely certain of, it was that Alex Bennett loved fiercely and he protected what he loved with everything he had. With that said, there was no doubt in Sam's mind that Alex was in love with Monica. God only knew how Monica felt about that or if she even knew.

The door to Monica's office was closed. She sat at her desk staring at yet another prettily wrapped box. This is what she'd been doing for the past ten minutes.

Her meeting with Karena had been taken in Karena's office because Monica didn't want to be bombarded with calls and interruptions until she was finished. When it looked as if everything on Karena's end was under control Monica headed to her office.

It was after two o'clock and she was feeling light-headed since she had yet to have lunch. She had stopped at Adonna's desk, picked up messages and listened to her assistant give her the rundown of what had happened since she left.

"And this guy, his name's Yates Hinton, he called about a million times. He just kept asking for you over and over again, wanting to know when you'd be back, where you were. It was weird."

"Yes," Monica said, keeping her eyes focused on the messages she flipped through even though she wasn't reading one word that had been written. "Weird."

"He even came in one day and dropped off a package for you. That was beyond weird because he'd just called, like, two hours ago and then he shows up."

Monica lifted her head. "He was here?" she asked slowly. He'd been in her house and now he'd been to her office. She had to put a stop to this.

Adonna nodded. "I told him I don't know how many times that I didn't know when you were returning or where you'd gone. Finally I had to call Karena. I hope you don't mind."

"No. Don't worry about it, Adonna. I'll handle him."

"So you do know him? I wasn't sure since he's not in your contacts. Karena didn't seem to know him so I was almost positive he wasn't some long-lost relative."

Adonna could talk for hours, this Monica already knew and didn't appreciate on a normal day. Today, with her head throbbing, her eyes feeling scratchy from getting zero sleep last night and her stomach growling, Monica couldn't stand it at all.

"Adonna," she said, trying valiantly not to yell and risk splitting her head right in two, "it's all right. I'll take care of Mr. Hinton. If he calls again, put him through."

"Oh, okay, Ms. Lakefield."

"I'll take these messages and start making callbacks. Can you order me a tuna on wheat toast with lettuce and a diet soda?"

"Sure, no problem."

That was a lie, Monica thought as she moved to her office. Her life was full of problems. One of which she was getting ready to confront.

Now, ten minutes later she was still sitting in the exact same spot she'd fallen into the moment she saw the box.

She should just open it, see what it was then throw it out, just like she'd done with the rabbit. Or rather, like Karena did with the rabbit last night.

"To hell with this," she said, picking up the box and dropping it into the trash can beside her desk. It didn't fit and the box and the trash can fell over.

She cursed just as Adonna buzzed into her office.

"Yes?" she answered tersely.

"Yates Hinton on line two."

Monica froze. Bent over, arms extended, hands reaching for the trash can and the box. "Fine. I'll take it," she replied.

As she sat up in her chair she took a deep, steadying breath and looked at the phone. One of her lines blinked red. On, off, on, off. It was Yates Hinton. The man she had thought she loved and knew now that she hated.

She reached out, grabbed the receiver and punched the button next to the blinking light.

"Monica Lakefield," she said in her coolest business-like voice.

"It's so nice to hear your voice again, Bunny."

She couldn't say the same to him. It wasn't nice to

hear him again. It was eerie and inappropriate and just damned irritating.

"What do you want, Yates?" she asked simply. There was no need for niceties.

"I want what I've always wanted. You."

"That's over and done with. Can I do something else for you?"

"Did you like the gift I left at your house?"

"Breaking and entering is so unlike you. I thought you Southerners were bred with better manners."

"I delivered one to your office, too. Have you opened it yet?"

"No," she said then felt a chill ripple down her spine.

"I don't want any gifts from you, Yates. And while we're on the subject, you can stop calling my office. We have nothing to talk about."

"But you're wrong. We have lots to talk about," Yates said seriously.

"Like what?"

"Like that man you're seeing."

Her heart thumped and Monica swallowed. She rested her elbows on the desk, held the phone with one hand and pinched the bridge of her nose with the other. "I'm not seeing anyone."

"Oh, but you are. And I know who he is."

She didn't say a word.

"Do you remember what I told you before you left South Carolina, Bunny?"

She was shaking her head but didn't speak.

"I told you I'd kill you before seeing you with anyone else."

"Yates," she said, her voice an achy croak.

"The thought of him putting his hands on you has

made me sick these past couple of days. I can't eat or sleep from wanting to rip his throat out."

His voice had changed, too. It was high-pitched and the Southern drawl was all but lost. He sounded almost frantic.

"I don't owe you any explanations. Why don't you just go home to your wife?"

"Don't do that, Bunny. Don't try to bring her into this. Roslyn has nothing to do with us."

"There is no us, Yates. Remember? Because there is a Roslyn. You were married the entire time we were together. You lied to me and you hurt me."

"It wasn't intentional. I told you that."

"I don't give a damn what you told me. You lied and you betrayed me. So I don't have anything else to say to you. Ever!"

Monica slammed the phone down and sat back in her chair. It rolled a little with the action and she let her arms fall to her lap. "Dammit. Dammit. Dammit!" she screamed then kicked the box until it skittered across the floor and slammed into the wall.

Chapter 19

Alex heard the noise as he lifted his hand to knock on Monica's office door. So instead of knocking he opened the door and walked inside, only to stop just short of a rolling trash can coming his way. He dropped a foot down on the runaway trash can, stopping it in its trek.

"Hello," he said, looking at Monica with a half smile. "Having a bad day?"

"Wondering why I was in such a rush to come back from Aspen," she mumbled. "Sorry."

Alex closed the door, picked up the trash can and walked toward her desk. He put the trash can down beside it and continued to where Monica was sitting, turning the chair so that she could face him.

"Tell me what's going on, Queen."

"Please, Alex, not today. My name is Monica."

She sighed and looked everywhere but at him. Alex

stood up, slipped his hands into his pockets and continued to stare at her.

"The way I see it is you can voluntarily tell me about this Yates Hinton and why he's sending you gifts you obviously don't want and calling you like it's a life-or-death emergency. Or I can keep digging until I find out what I need to know to get this fool out of your life."

Despite Sam's warning Alex knew how best to deal with Monica. She would definitely detest him investigating behind her back. But telling her up front what his intentions were and giving her the opportunity to tell him herself to back off would allow her to feel as if she still had some control. Even though he had no intention of listening to her about not getting involved. She was a part of his life now, a more important part than he'd thought just a few weeks ago. So she was going to have to deal with his interfering just like the rest of the people in his life that he loved.

"Karena has a big mouth," she said. She tried to stand, but he wouldn't move out of her way so they ended up closer than she probably wanted.

"Not Karena. Sam. When I told him about our issues in Aspen he told me about the guy desperately trying to get in contact with you back here. It's logical to put two and two together."

"It's logical to let me handle my own life," she said, using her palms to push against his chest in an attempt to move him.

But Alex wasn't going to be moved. He grabbed both her wrists and when she struggled he simply lifted her hands to his lips and kissed each of her knuckles.

"We all need help sometimes. If this was one of your

sisters you'd be doing exactly what I'm doing. So calm down and tell me about this guy so I can help."

Her lips pressed together so tightly Alex thought they'd remain that way. Damn, she was one beautiful woman, especially when she was angry.

"You can't help. Even if I tell you he's a past mistake, the biggest one of my life, there's nothing you can do to stop his current harassment."

Okay, at least she wasn't pushing back at him anymore. "Why's he harassing you now? Does he want you back?"

"He never wanted me to leave."

And that statement had Alex battling an array of emotions—jealousy, anger, fury.

"So why did you leave him?"

He let her pull her arms away from him and she sat back down in the chair. "Because he was married."

Alex sat on the edge of her desk. "Did you know this when you started seeing him?"

"Of course not!" she retorted, looking at him as if he should have known that.

"I apologize. I knew the answer here," he said, touching a hand over his heart, "but needed to hear it anyway."

"It doesn't matter. It was a long time ago."

"When you were in college?"

"Yes."

"He went to school with you?"

"He taught at the college. We started seeing each other then I found out he was married and ended it. Case closed," she said with finality.

"For you but not for him."

"I don't give a damn what he thinks, Alex. I told him

back then that I didn't want to have anything more to do with him and I just told him again a few minutes before you walked in. It's over and that's that."

But Hinton obviously didn't feel that way. And, as it went with stalkers, her telling Yates to stop wasn't going to be enough to keep the guy away. Alex kept that tidbit of info to himself.

"Have you had lunch?"

She blinked at him then sighed. "Adonna ordered me a sandwich."

He nodded. "Then I'll stay while you eat then you can show me around your gallery."

"Alex, I have a lot of catching up to do today."

He raised a brow. "My mother loves art. My brother is a sculptor. Do you really want to deny me a tour?"

One elegantly arched eyebrow lifted as she asked, "Using your family name and connections to get what you want, Mr. Bennett?"

Alex shrugged. "By any means necessary."

She smiled and all the anger and jealousy inside Alex melted away. This was what it was all about, Monica's happiness. Whatever he had to do to guarantee that he would, regardless of what she or anyone else said.

"And this is where I'd like to feature your brother Lorenzo," Monica was saying as she and Alex entered the first-floor alcove, which housed the more risqué pieces.

"Warning—if you call him Lorenzo you're never going to get him to show his pieces here," Alex said as he walked around the room. "It's kind of small in here."

"That's because we haven't secured Renny's pieces yet. Once we do we plan to merge this room with the two on either side to accommodate a larger showing. We'd also have a special event announcing his work is here. He's picked up a huge following in the last two years and the Lakefield Galleries would like to show our support for him, as well."

Alex nodded. He was looking at an oil painting of two lovers, African-American, on a white backdrop. The bodies were nude on a red couch, the position explicit and alluring, tasteful in a sensual way and enticingly erotic. Secretly, it was one of Monica's favorites. Judging by the way Alex was staring at it, he was enjoying it, too.

"That's by an artist named Zune. He's fantastic with oils," she told him.

Alex nodded. "He's fantastic, all right. This is one realistic portrait."

Was it hot in here? Or had the deepening of Alex's voice simply jacked the heat up?

She cleared her throat. "You like it?"

He turned to her. "I do. You like it, Monica?"

He'd used her name and not Queen as he usually referred to her. She licked her lips and concentrated on keeping her eyes trained on his.

"I do."

Alex took a step closer to her, touching the palm of his hand to her cheek. "What do you like about it?"

Monica's nipples tingled beneath the thin coral camisole she wore beneath her black suit jacket. "I like the imagery, the way he uses stark colors to portray the sensual air in the room. Sometimes an artist will use dark colors to portray romance and sexuality. But Zune goes for the opposite, the bright to accentuate the obvious. It's fantastic."

"You accentuate the obvious," he said, his thumb brushing over her gloss-coated lips.

"We were talking about the painting," she said. As she opened her mouth to speak her tongue swiped the pad of his thumb.

His eyes darkened, lust clearly taking hold. With his free hand he pulled her to him. "I'm talking about you and I creating our own erotic scene."

"Alex, I'm at work," she said breathlessly.

"Queen, I'm falling in love with you," he whispered before his lips touched hers, pulling her into a deep, heated kiss.

She loved his kisses, absolutely craved them when he wasn't around. Who would have known a man could kiss like this, in a way that had her knees going weak and her center pulsating. As her eyes closed she saw clearly the erotic scene they could create, whether on a kitchen counter, in a bathtub full of bubbles or in a hotel room. It was like fire with them. Fire in the midst of winter, kisses that heated, devoured and destroyed.

"Monica!" The stern voice broke their contact instantly.

Monica knew that voice and she knew the person it belonged to was beyond pissed. Turning slowly, she faced her father, Paul Lakefield.

"If you have a moment to spare from your...activities," Paul Lakefield said in the stern way he was used to talking, "I would like you to explain this package I just received."

Straightening her back the way she always seemed to do when confronted, Monica cleared her throat. "Hello,

Dad. This is Alexander Bennett of Bennett Industries. You know, the communications—"

Paul cut her off. "I know all about Bennett Industries. Marvin and I have been longtime business associates. It's nice to meet the son who'll be taking his place as head of the company soon. I can only hope you have your father's dedication to the business," Paul said, extending a hand to Alex but giving him a less than confident look.

Alex smiled and reached for Mr. Lakefield's hand. He knew of Paul Lakefield, as well, from both his father's mention of the man and Sam and Max's briefing about the father. "It's a pleasure to meet you, sir. I can assure you that Bennett Industries will be in good hands when I take over. Monica was just showing me your gallery. It's a great collection of art, sir."

"Never mind what my daughter was showing you, Mr. Bennett. We have a private matter to discuss, so if you'll excuse us."

"You can say what you have to say in front of Alex," Monica intervened to Alex's pleasure and surprise.

"I said it's private," Paul insisted.

Alex reached for Monica's hand. She laced her fingers through his in a show of solidarity. "Alex is a personal friend, Dad. It's okay to talk around him."

A personal friend. Alex figured that was better than nothing at all. Would he have liked for her to say he was her man, her lover or something of that nature? Sure. But that would be pushing Monica too fast, too soon. He'd accept what he could get, for now.

"Fine. What is this?" Paul asked, thrusting an envelope toward Monica.

She reached for it and pulled out the contents. Her

gasp had Alex holding her hand even tighter as he looked over to see what she'd seen.

They were pictures of a much younger Monica, a much happier one, walking hand in hand with a man. Instinct told Alex this was Yates Hinton but he remained silent.

"Where did you get these?" she asked in a strangled voice.

"They were delivered to me just about a half hour ago, along with some sort of threat against the gallery," Paul replied.

"What type of threat?" Alex asked.

"The letter asks for Monica's resignation from the gallery because of moral conflicts," Paul informed them.

"What? Moral conflicts? What does that mean?" She'd leaned into Alex, probably inadvertently, but he was glad he was there to support her.

Paul frowned. "I was hoping you could explain that, Monica. What have you done?"

"Me?" she asked incredulously. "I haven't done anything except work my butt off for this gallery, for the Lakefield name. You know that's all I've done since I came back from college, Dad."

"Obviously you were doing something else while you were at college," Paul retorted.

Alex took the envelope and its contents out of Monica's hands. The pictures went from innocent walks to candlelight dinners, to a bedroom shot that could have been hanging on the wall right next to these other erotic paintings. A muscle in his jaw ticked as he reigned in his anger and strived for calm. Getting angry was not going to help deal with Mr. Lakefield, who was already plenty pissed off.

"This man has been harassing Monica, Mr. Lakefield. He's sending her unwanted gifts, calling her repeatedly making idle threats. This looks like he's trying to step up his game."

"And what game would that be, Mr. Bennett?" Paul asked, dragging his angry gaze from Monica to the man standing beside her.

"He's trying to intimidate her into coming back to him."

"Oh, God, why won't this go away?" Monica sighed. "It was years ago. I've moved on. He should, too."

But she hadn't moved on, not really. Alex knew that and he suspected Monica did, too, but now was neither the time nor place to discuss that.

"You were intimate with this man. So what? You broke up and he's still holding on. I understand that but how does that relate to a morality issue?" Paul inquired.

Alex didn't answer. It was Monica's story to tell, not his, even though he'd already been given a quick synopsis of what was going on in this chapter of the story.

"He was married when I was seeing him," she replied in a surprisingly strong and level voice, as if she dared her father to cast blame on her.

Paul sighed, running a hand down his face. It was then that Alex saw something he suspected Monica couldn't see. Her father was worried. He was angry about the pictures and the threat on the gallery—no matter how frivolous and inappropriate—and he was also worried about his child.

"Did you know?"

Monica sighed again. "I guess everybody who finds

out is going to ask me that question. No, I didn't know he was married. When I found out I ended it. But he's not letting go."

"It's been years since you left South Carolina—why is he surfacing now?" was Paul's next question.

Alex waited for that answer, as well.

"He thinks I'm seeing someone else."

Paul looked to Alex, who looked to Monica, wishing she'd told him this before.

"And he doesn't want you seeing anyone else, even though he's still married? Dumbass games men play," Paul said.

"It doesn't matter, Dad. I told him it was over between us. I told him not to bother me anymore."

"And yet he sent these to me anyway. He's threatening to slander the gallery's name, to contact all our contributors, our artists, to attack our credibility in the art world."

"He can't do that," Monica said, sounding horrified at the thought.

Paul shook his head. "I don't think he'll do much damage seeing as he's the one that was married at the time, not you. But it's a hit I don't want us to take, especially considering how close we are to expanding." Taking a deep breath, Paul looked directly at Monica. "I want you to take a leave of absence."

"What? Are you kidding? You're firing me because of this maniac?"

"Mr. Lakefield, with all due respect, sir, I don't think giving in to this guy is the way to go."

"And how do you think we should handle this, Mr. Bennett? Since it seems you're the man she's seeing now, how do you suppose I keep my company's name in good standing with this type of scandal looming over us?"

"I don't think it's that big of a deal. So she slept with a married man—it was almost ten years ago and she hasn't had any contact with him since then. These pictures seem bad but we could always claim they were altered. That's a normal occurrence nowadays. I think you should be looking to prosecute him for harassment instead. Fight back instead of backing down."

Paul shook his head again. "Young men, I tell you. You have the energy and gumption to suggest fighting back. Well, I'm a businessman and I'm thinking about my business."

"But what about your daughter? Did it occur to you that firing me plays right into his hands? He wants me vulnerable because he thinks that'll run me right back to him. Apparently he's been keeping close tabs on me. He had to if he found out about me and Alex when there wasn't even a me and Alex. If I'm not at the gallery it won't stop him, but it'll devastate me."

"I'm sorry, Monica. You'll have to deal with that on your own. And I'm not firing you. I'm simply asking you to take some time off, distance yourself from the gallery for a while."

"You want me to go away so you don't have to deal with me or the issues you believe I'm bringing to your precious gallery. Never mind that I'm the one who put the wheels in motion for the expansion to Miami and to Atlanta. I found the location, I personally interviewed the managers, I've been developing the marketing plans and searching out new artwork to show. I've worked my butt off for this expansion, for this gallery all my life and this is how you repay me? Well, thanks a lot, Dad. Thanks a whole helluva lot."

Alex let her hand go and she stormed out of the room. She needed to be alone to get herself together. Breaking down in front of her father was not an option for Monica. He got that. What he didn't get was Paul Lakefield's attitude toward a child he so obviously loved.

"She'll get over it," Paul said when it was just him and Alex.

"You sure about that, sir?"

"Are you questioning my judgment? I'm her father, for goodness' sake! I know what's best for her."

"I don't think you know her very well, Mr. Lakefield. And that's the real pity of this situation. She's your daughter and she's dedicated her life to pleasing you, but you can't see that. Or you're too stubborn and egotistical to acknowledge it."

"Now, wait a minute, young man. You might be sleeping with her, but I'm her father. I'm the man who raised her, who taught her everything she knows about this business."

"And you're the one who just broke her heart, again."

Alex left Paul Lakefield with those words to chew on as he headed to Monica's office.

He wasn't surprised to find the door closed, but it wasn't locked so he walked in. She was packing, throwing things from her desk into a box, tears streaming down her face.

Touching her wasn't going to be a good idea even though all Alex wanted to do right now was hold her. She'd rebel and push him away, so he didn't bother.

"I'll take you home," he said instead.

"I can get a cab."

"You can, but I'm here so I'll take you."

She looked up at him as if she was going to argue but stopped. "I can't believe this is happening. I want to kill Yates Hinton, that bastard!"

Alex nodded, knowing exactly how she felt. "Let's just get you home then we'll figure out what to do about Yates Hinton."

But Alex had already figured it out and while he'd walked to Monica's office from the lower level of the gallery he'd sent Sam Desdune a text message letting him know what his plan was.

Chapter 20

Alex parked in the garage located on the first two floors of Monica's apartment building. On the elevator up he held her hand even though she didn't want him to. He was good at doing things she didn't want. And she was getting even better at letting him.

It had been so easy to lean on Alex today and Monica figured it was a good thing he was there. What would she have done differently if he wasn't? Nothing, probably. Still, she liked that she'd been able to lean on him when her father had read her the riot act. And as much as it went against the kind of woman she'd tried desperately to become, she liked that he was here with her now.

As she let herself into the apartment, she watched with dismal disinterest as Alex moved about the apartment ahead of her. She knew what he was looking for—

another box from Yates, a letter, pictures, anything that would show the man had been inside her place again. Her heart hammered in her chest the entire time he moved around, but she went to the couch and sat down instead of following him.

She was tired, so tired of carrying all these secrets and living this life of the strong, undefeatable, unobtainable Monica Lakefield. Now what she really wanted to do was go someplace and sleep, finally sleep restfully in some quiet locale away from all that was stressful in her life. The ringing phone beside her startled her right out of that reverie.

Alex was back in the room eyeing her closely. Monica looked at the caller ID. "It says unavailable."

"I'm going to ask Sam to put a tracing device on the phone but he can't get into the city for another hour or two. Go ahead and answer it."

She nodded and picked up the cordless phone from its base. "Hello?" she answered tentatively.

"Hello?" Monica repeated when there was no answer.

"Hang up. He's just toying with you," Alex told her.

But Monica didn't listen. She wanted to hear Yates's voice, wanted another chance to tell him where to go and how fast he could get there. "Hello?" she yelled into the phone just before Alex took it out of her hand and pushed the off button.

"He's going to keep trying to get to you, Queen. You've got to be one step ahead of him. Now," he said, sitting on the couch next to her. "When Sam gets here he'll put the trace on your phone and place another agent downstairs in the lobby."

"Another one?" she asked.

"Yes, he's had a guy down there since I left here last night."

"But Yates had already been here."

"Unfortunately, that's true. But now we have Yates's name and a current picture Sam got from his DMV records. If he shows up here they'll know and they'll catch him."

Monica nodded, sitting back on the couch and letting her head fall back. She closed her eyes, trying to push this mess out of her mind. But it wasn't working—she was thinking about her job, about the gallery opening in Miami in the fall, about her sisters and her parents.

"Why didn't you tell me he was coming after you because of me?" she heard Alex ask.

"I didn't know until today when he called," she answered but didn't open her eyes.

"So he's been following you all along, taking pictures and watching what you do with your life. I guess for the last few years your self-induced single life made him damn happy."

She shrugged. "I guess it did."

"And now he believes you've found somebody else, that you've moved on to love without him."

"I don't know what's going on in his head. He's crazy and unpredictable."

"He's damn smart to have figured us for a couple even before we became one."

Her eyes did open then. "Are we a couple, Alex? I mean, really, we spent a few nights together because our families set us up. If we'd stayed here would we have been at this point? Would Yates have even come out of the woodwork?"

"He knew before we went to Aspen, Queen. The fact

that we were away together probably pushed him closer to the edge. We're both relatively well-known in this area and your sister just married a Donovan, a family who are almost like royalty in the African-American communities across the world. If he was keeping tabs on you all this time he would have definitely seen us together before Aspen."

"I know." She sighed. "But we weren't a couple then."

"But we are now," he countered.

His words seemed quiet in the room and Monica closed her eyes again. "I don't know what we are or what we're not. All I know for sure is that I'm jobless and confused and tired of all this crap."

Alex took her hand in his. "When it's all over I'll take you to a secluded beach where you can get some rest."

"Are you going to tranquilize me? You know I don't sleep at night."

"I think once you let go of the anxiety of your past, once you're sure Yates is in your past, you'll be able to sleep just fine. Besides, every night that I've been in bed with you, you've slept like a baby."

And that was the truth. That night they'd spent at the inn she'd slept curled in his arms throughout the entire night. He'd had to wake her up in the morning to get ready for their flight. She'd even slept through the New Year because Alex was beside her.

"I don't know what we're doing, Alex," she admitted finally. "I swore I'd never get involved with another man. After Yates it just all seemed like a waste of my time."

"How did you find out he was married?"

"His wife found out about me. Actually, I think she always knew he had affairs. At least that's what she told me when she called me to their house. She said he liked to pick young women at the college, that he didn't want a woman his age or an older woman, for that matter. His wife's older than he is by five years. She's an heiress to a sugarcane fortune or something like that. Anyway, it wasn't a surprise to her. And that's what I don't understand. If this was part of Yates's routine, why didn't he just move on to another girl when I left?"

"You're not an easy woman to forget, Queen."

He'd said it so simply, so sincerely, she looked at him and almost smiled. Alex, her hero, still wearing his navy-blue dress pants and stark white dress shirt and blue-and-white paisley-print tie that he'd most likely worn to work this morning.

"Oh, I almost forgot. How did your meeting go? You didn't miss it because of me, did you?"

He smiled. "No. I moved the time of the meeting up because I wanted to come into the city to spend the evening with a beautiful woman. Everything went fine. We're all set for the launch. I've done more interviews and posed for more pictures than I ever care to again in this lifetime but it'll all be worth it."

"Yes, it will. Bennett Industries will be a bigger success then it already is. I believe that."

"I'm glad you believe it because I didn't want to be the only one wishing for its success."

She shook her head. "Never. I want only the best for you, Alex."

"And I want you for me," he said, leaning closer and resting his forehead against hers.

"I'm not so sure that's best," she whispered.

* * *

In the car parked in the garage Yates slammed his hands on the steering wheel.

That slickster was with her!

He'd waited in this garage for Monica to return home from work only to be angered when he saw her getting out of a gray Mercedes with that man. Oh, he knew who the man was, Alexander Bennett, prince of the Bennett fortune. He looked like a foreigner with his inky-black hair and smooth light brown skin. Yates had done thorough research on the Bennetts. The mother was from Brazil, a pretty enough woman with exotic looks and a regal air to her. She'd married simply enough, a thriving black businessman who built an empire for her and their five children. Alex was next in line to inherit everything from his father. That alone made Yates despise him.

He hated the rich, the ones who were born into privilege and carried it around like crowns on their heads. His own parents had been blue-collar workers—his mother sewed zippers into dresses at a small factory in Gilbert, South Carolina. His father worked as a runner at the local drugstore until his legs couldn't carry him anymore. They'd both died as poor as the day they were born. That's when Yates had changed his name from Hinton Beauford and moved out of Gilbert. The new identity gave him a chance to be something his parents never cared to work for, a success. The first part of that success was going to college on a scholarship he'd received for running like the wind in high school. Back then it was beyond astonishing to see a skinny little black boy run faster than the milkman's truck could drive. Yates had parlayed that scholarship into a degree, then a master's and had used his Southern charm to court the richest woman in town, Roslyn Smith, heiress to Smith Sugarcane.

Marrying Roslyn and being on staff at the college gave Yates money and prestige. But Roslyn was a cold older woman with no intention of ever changing. Yates needed more and found it in the fresh young faces that came to the college. He'd hit pay dirt with Monica Lakefield, who had something none of the other girls before her did.

Monica was beautiful, there was no doubt, and Yates was immediately attracted to her sleek, sexy body. But beyond that she was intelligent and she came from a good family that started out in South Carolina, as well. The Lakefields were rich and getting richer, and Monica was going to work for her daddy the minute she graduated college. That was all she could talk about.

So Yates wanted her and her money immediately. And for years he'd had her. Until Roslyn found out and destroyed any bit of happiness Yates could have had.

He'd never forgotten Monica, never would. He was determined to keep her with him one way or another. If he hadn't let Roslyn and her drunken threats keep him from Monica this time, he wasn't about to let this pretty rich boy do it.

After climbing out of his car, Yates went to the truck and pulled out a bag. Then he grabbed his cell phone and made a call. "I need you here at Monica's building right now."

There were some excuses and some background noise on the line that Yates didn't have time to decipher.

"Just get your ass down here now before I make you sorry you ever took my money!"

Snapping the phone closed, he put the bag on his shoulders and slammed the trunk closed.

Monica's little boyfriend was going to be more than sorry he'd ever touched what belonged to Yates, that was for damn sure.

Chapter 21

"We're going out to dinner," Alex said, following her into the bedroom.

Sam was in the living room putting some contraption onto her phone. She'd wanted a moment alone to get away from the probing eyes of each man and the possible thoughts going through their head about her relationship with Yates.

"I'm really not in the mood to go out, Alex."

"Come on," he said, threading his arms around her waist and pulling her back against him. "Are you really willing to keep hiding from this guy, to keep living this sheltered life to keep him at bay?"

"That's not what I've been doing. I just didn't want to go through it all over again, the betrayal, the lies, the…"

"The shame. I know what it must have done to you

to find out he was married. You trusted him, believed in him, probably thought you were in love with him. But, Monica, what you need to understand was that all of this was Yates's fault. He was older, more mature. He had a wife and a responsibility to her, to his job. He pushed all that aside to toy with an innocent young woman. What happened was his fault, not yours."

She listened to his words and knew there was truth to them.

"How is going out to dinner tonight of all nights making that better?"

"It's showing him that he hasn't beaten you. He didn't all those years ago because you came back to New York and made a name for yourself and for your father's company. Going out tonight will show him you're better than him again."

"What's in it for you?" she asked.

"Me? What makes you think I have an ulterior motive?"

She shifted in his arms so she could see him. "I just have a feeling you and Sam cooked this dinner up long before you came in here with me."

He smiled, looking into the brown eyes he'd come to love and hearing the voice that made him want to get down on his knees and beg her to marry him.

"My family's coming and so are yours. We'll have a nice family dinner then come back here so you can get some sleep."

"Both our families? Are you crazy? You saw how my father acted today. I'm the last person he wants to see."

"You're the first person he wants to see because he wants to make sure you're all right."

When she started to protest he stopped her. "You think your father only looks at you with business eyes. I suspect your sisters think he looks at them with less than pleasing thoughts, as well, because you're all girls. But today, I saw something different in your father. He's worried, Queen. Worried that this man might hurt you, that he might hurt what you've worked so hard to create. Sure, he showed it badly today but I think he was trying to do what he thought was right."

"I don't think you were looking at my father. But because my head is hurting too much to keep this argument going I'm going to shower and change. Then we'll go out to dinner. I'd tell you to do the same but your place is too far away."

"Never fear, Sam brought some of my clothes by when he came."

Narrowing her eyes at him as she pulled out of his embrace, Monica quipped, "Yeah, you had this planned all along."

Alex's reply was a deep chuckle and a warm feeling inside that the woman he was desperately in love with was about to meet his family.

Gabriella Bennett was a cheerful beauty with her long curly hair and big smile. Adriana was stunning, tall, leggy, busty, every man's dream. Rico had a cool air to him, but when he smiled she saw the twinkle of humor in his eyes. Renny was definitely gorgeous, in the *GQ* magazine sort of way and he loved his wife, the petite but boisterous Bree, to pieces.

Sam was Sam and Karena was Karena, both grinning wildly at any mention of their pending parenthood. The elder Bennetts were just as in love as Monica thought they probably were the day they first met. When she looked down to the end of the table where her parents were seated, Monica thought that perhaps if she'd been meeting Paul and Noreen for the first time she would think the same about them. But this wasn't the first time she'd seen her parents together so it was different to see her father taking her mother's hand and kissing its back as they laughed about a memory Noreen had just shared with the elder Bennetts.

"See, not as bad as you thought," Alex whispered to her.

"Score one for you, but this doesn't mean anything. We're just having dinner," she was saying when he kissed her lips.

"Alex," she scolded.

"That's my boy," Marvin Bennett said. "Never been afraid to take what he wanted."

"I'll warn him now to be careful with my daughter," Paul said with a chuckle.

Monica couldn't believe what she was hearing and seeing. This wasn't her father. It wasn't the man who'd just hours ago fired her.

"So, Monica, I hear you're opening a gallery in Miami later this year," Adriana said after sipping from her wine.

Monica looked at her father, who gave her a nod to proceed. "Yes, we are. We were very fortunate for the help of my mother's business partner, Alma Donovan, who referred us to DNM, Donovan Network Management. They're based in Miami and have a great staff of agents in the entertainment, literary and art industries. Through them I was able to hire a manager and freelance a few scouts for the opening. We're very excited about the expansion."

"So is Alex, he couldn't stop talking about all your accolades when he came over yesterday morning," Adriana said, looking toward her brother. "I hope you don't find this too forward of me, but seeing as we're probably going to be family soon, I was wondering if you could refer me to an agent at DNM."

Ignoring her remark about them becoming family, Monica nodded agreeably. "Of course. I have Jaydon Donovan's number on speed dial. She manages DNM and would be glad to help you out."

"Thanks, I really appreciate it."

"No problem." Monica stopped quickly because she'd almost said that's what family does for each other.

They weren't family, not officially. And maybe not ever. This thing between her and Alex wasn't etched in stone. Hell, she didn't even know what this thing between them was.

Dinner proceeded without a hitch and before she knew it they were back at her apartment.

"I really enjoyed meeting your family," she said after Alex helped remove her coat and hung it in the closet with his own.

"They enjoyed meeting you. And your father was on his best behavior. Weren't you proud?"

Monica chuckled. "Yes, I was. You know what he said to me after dinner?"

"No. What?"

"He pulled me to the side and apologized for hurting my feelings. He said he was only doing what he thought was best to protect me. I've never thought my father would protect me from anything."

"That's because you think you're the only one capable of doing the protecting."

He'd taken her hand and was walking her to the bedroom.

"You're right. I used to think that."

"And how hard was it for you to just admit I was right?"

"Very hard," she said, smiling up at him as he pulled her into his arms.

"But I thank you anyway for giving me that much at least. Let's go to bed," Alex whispered.

"You're staying?"

"Of course I'm staying. Until this maniac is caught and maybe long after that."

"Don't be ridiculous, Alex. You have your own place and your own life in Connecticut. Moving here with me isn't logical."

"Being away from you isn't an option."

She could have argued more, but Monica really didn't have the strength. Besides, she realized she'd love nothing more than to curl up next to Alex tonight and sleep. Finally.

But sleep wasn't meant to be for Monica.

In the dead of night her cell phone, which she'd put on vibrate when she was at the restaurant, skidded across her nightstand. She reached for it the minute she heard it break through the silence of the room.

"Hello?" she whispered, her voice hoarse from sleep.

"If you want your little boyfriend to stay alive you'll meet me on the first floor. Now."

The message was quick and to the point. The hang-up was rude and deliberately designed to piss her off. So as she crept slowly out of the bed she was already thinking of the choice words she would have for Mr. Hinton the minute she saw him. How dare he threaten her again? And now he was threatening Alex? That was completely unacceptable.

Monica had slipped on some sweatpants and a shirt and had made it all the way out into the living room when something told her to be prepared. She went into the kitchen and grabbed a knife from the drawer, then looked down for a place she could conceal it.

She'd never had to hurt anyone in her life. Except for that night a year ago when she'd clobbered that guy who'd attacked Deena. That was self-defense. And if Yates got out of hand this time, as he'd done in the past, she was going to defend herself like she never had before.

Chapter 22

Monica stepped off the elevator at the first-floor parking garage. She moved slowly, looking around the brightly lit cement-floored area. She saw what she normally saw when she entered this floor—cars.

No Yates.

Taking a few more steps, she kept her eyes and ears open. She'd stuffed the knife in the elastic band of her pants and was walking a bit stiffly so as not to stab herself in the leg. It was chilly down here and she'd neglected to put on a jacket.

She was about to turn back and go upstairs when he grabbed her from behind.

"Hey, Bunny," he whispered right into her ear, his voice raspy, his breath hot.

"Let go of me, Yates."

"Not yet," he said, moaning as his arms tightened

around her, his arousal pressing into her back. "I've been thinking about holding you again for so long, Bunny. So, so long."

"I'm not your bunny and I don't want you touching me," she said, squirming to get free of his grasp.

"You don't try to get away from him, do you? You let him hold you and touch you. I hate that, Bunny. You know I hate the thought of any man touching you."

Monica kicked back, finally catching his shin with the heel of her shoe. "Let go!" she yelled and tumbled free of his grasp when he groaned and leaned down to rub his leg.

Yates had always been soft—why she hadn't seen that before she didn't know. She only wore tennis shoes, not her usual heels that may have cut into his skin if she kicked him. Yet he was bent over whining like a baby.

"Why don't you go back to your wife?"

"I want you."

"Well, I don't want you," she spat.

"Who do you want, Monica? Is it that pretty boy you've got sleeping in your bed? Is he loving you like I did? Is he making you feel like a woman the way I did?"

She wanted to puke, right then and there she just wanted to vomit all over him for saying such a vile and ridiculous thing. If he thought what he'd done to her had made her feel like a woman he was more pitiful than she'd first suspected.

"He makes me feel nothing like you did."

"That's why you need to come back to me," he said, taking a step toward her.

Monica backed up and felt herself stopping when her backside hit a car. This looked nothing like the man she'd left in South Carolina. He looked older, sadder, if that were possible. The hair that was just barely sprinkled with gray was now full-blown salt-and-pepper and his beard was rough, not neatly cropped as he'd worn it before. But what really worried her were his eyes. They looked crazy, deranged and they almost danced around, dark excitable orbs that had her taking a deep steadying breath.

"I'll never come back to you, Yates. Even if I end things with Alex, I still won't come back to you."

He licked his lips, his hands fisting at his sides. "You remember what I told you that night before you snuck off."

Oh, God, did she remember that night. Each and every day, each time the sky turned indigo and the lights in her apartment went out she remembered. That night alone had been the sole reason sleep evaded her on a regular basis.

"That will never happen again. Never. And I don't give a damn what you said."

"Oh, you remember and you do give a damn," he said, giving her a crooked smile. "I told you what I'd do to you if I couldn't have you, Bunny."

"Stop calling me that!" she yelled. Hearing it pushed her right back to that night, all those years ago, when he'd said it over and over again.

"But you are my Bunny. You'll always be my Bunny."

"No!" Monica closed her eyes and tried to block out the sound.

Then he was on her, his tall body, which had gained considerable weight since the last time she'd seen him, pressed her back into the car.

"Yates! No!" she cried out even as he groped her, whispering "Bunny" repeatedly in her ear. Just like he'd done that night.

Monica was about to scream again, about to reach for her knife and cut his black heart out, but Yates was suddenly pulled off of her and thrown to the ground.

"You okay?" Alex asked, standing there in just a pair of sweatpants and shoes.

Monica had never been so happy to see someone in her life. She swallowed the tears stinging her eyes and nodded.

But Yates wasn't down for the count. He jumped up with an agility she'd sworn a man of his fifty-two years couldn't have and gripped Alex in a headlock. It was then that Monica saw the gun.

"Yates, please. Please don't do this," she said, remembering those same words falling from her lips years ago.

"He won't have you, Bunny. He can't. He doesn't love you like I do."

"But I don't love you, Yates. I don't."

"Just go, Monica. I'll handle this. You just go," Alex told her, his eyes glaring at her. He wasn't fighting Yates, just staying slack in his grasp. Why wasn't he fighting back? He could whip Yates's ass—she knew he could. But if he wouldn't she definitely would.

"You will love me again. You will. Now, go down there and get in my car. I'll take care of him and then we'll be together again. Together, you and me, Bunny, again," Yates continued to chant as if she and Alex were not really there.

Monica was shaking her head. "No. No. Not this

time." Yates would not take another thing from her. Not again.

She reached into the band of her pants just as Yates began to turn, pulling Alex with him. Monica didn't think another minute, didn't second-guess herself, only moved with a quickness she'd later wonder how she managed. But she brought the knife down into the back of Yates's neck with as much power as she could manage.

He made a sound that reminded her of an injured animal. His body went stiff and Alex slipped from his grasp, catching the gun as it began to fall from Yates's hand. Alex immediately grabbed Monica, pulling her back from Yates's body and pushing her behind him.

Peering around Alex, she watched Yates fall to his knees. Still yelling, "Bunny. You'll always be my Bunny."

She was crying in earnest now, gut-wrenching sobs that brought her to her knees as his voice echoed in her ears.

Seconds later Alex heard the police sirens, saw Sam and his two men running from the elevator, guns drawn. He was on his knees lifting Monica's limp body into his arms. She was crying and the sound she made picked at his heart like a sharp blade.

The moment she had closed the door to the apartment he had woken up. It had taken him a few minutes to get dressed and call down to Miguel at the front desk to ask if he'd seen her leave. Miguel had told him no but that the cameras in the parking garage had picked her up stepping off the elevator. He'd gone there immediately and almost died a very slow, torturous death when he saw that man on top of Monica.

"You two okay?" Sam asked.

"She stabbed him" was all Alex said before walking toward the elevator, carrying Monica to safety.

The next morning Monica awoke to the smell of coffee brewing and a headache that threatened to bring her to tears one more time. She walked to the bathroom on legs that felt tired and achy. As she stood in front of the mirror after closing the door, she almost screamed of fright.

Her face was splotchy, her eyes swollen, puffy and red. She switched on the shower to the hottest water possible, then stripped off her nightgown and climbed in. The water burned her skin and she picked up the soap and began to scrub. Memories assailed her and she scrubbed harder and harder, trying desperately to rinse away the filth, the scum that had touched her, had defiled her.

Monica wasn't aware that she'd started crying or that she'd begun to scream until Alex pulled back the shower curtain and glared at her.

"What the hell are you doing?" he said, turning off the water and grabbing the soap from her hands.

"Stop it! Give it back—I have to wash. I have to be clean again. Don't you understand I have to be clean again? Like I was when I first came here."

She was still crying and still talking as Alex lifted her out of the shower and carried her into the bedroom.

"Sit right there," he told her before he disappeared back into the bathroom.

Monica sat there, rocking back and forth, rubbing her hands up and down her arms, still feeling as if something was crawling all over her—as if his filthy hands and lips were all over her again.

When Alex came back he held two towels, one he wrapped around her hair and the other he used to dry her skin. Tears continued to flow and her chest kept heaving. She hadn't cried like this in years, hadn't emptied everything she felt into tears in much too long.

"Baby, it's okay. He can't hurt you anymore. It's over. He's gone."

"He's gone?" She looked at him through blury eyes. "I ki-kil— I killed him?"

"No, Queen. But he's injured badly. He's in surgery right now to repair his spinal cord or something like that. But as soon as he's out of the hospital he'll be arrested and taken to jail. He won't hurt you again, baby. Never again."

"My name is Monica. Monica! Can't you say Monica?" she yelled, lifting her hands to cover her ears.

Calmly, Alex wrapped the towel around her and lifted her onto his lap. He pulled her hands from her ears and kissed her cheek. "I can say Monica just fine."

"Don't!" she screamed. "Just don't touch me anymore!" She was off his lap and walking across the floor in a flash. Monica tried to stand up straight but her legs wouldn't allow it; her body was just too damn tired. She did manage a deep breath and wiped at the tears that still streaked her face. "You know, Alex, there's a reason why I've been fighting you all this time. Fighting against this thing growing between us."

"Tell me the reason, Monica."

"I thought I could keep the secret. I thought I'd just tell everybody a little bit and then I could move on. But you know what?" she asked and turned to face him. "I can't. I can't keep going on with this on my mind. It haunts me every day. It stands between us every time you touch me, every time you look at me like you could possibly love me. It's there."

"What did he do to you?" Alex asked somberly.

Monica just stared at him. She looked at this man who worked hard for a living, who loved his family and his friends, who dealt with all her crap when a lesser man would have told her where to go and drawn a map so she could get there quickly. He looked tired, as if he hadn't slept, either. He wore jeans and a button-down shirt and he sat on her bed, his arms resting on his lap as he waited for what, he had no idea.

She owed him this, owed herself this one final truth.

"He raped me," she said slowly. She took a deep breath and repeated, "Yates Hinton raped me."

Monica saw the muscle twitch in his jaw, saw his hands fist and rushed to finish. "The night I left his house he came to my apartment. He'd signed a lease for me and was paying the monthly rent so we could stop meeting at the hotel and we wouldn't be seen at the dorm. He was angry that I'd accepted his wife's invitation to the house, angrier when I said it was over between us. He threatened to have me thrown out of school, but it was too late for that. I already had all my credits to graduate.

"When it didn't look like I was going to change my mind, I guess Yates just figured this was the next best thing to crushing me."

"Monica, you don't have to continue," Alex said, standing and taking a step toward her.

"Yes, I do," she said, holding up a hand to warn him away from her. "I have to do this for both of us. You think you know me but you don't really, not until I tell you everything."

Alex slipped his hands in his pockets, she suspected because he didn't know what else to do with them. If she'd let him approach her he would have held her, cuddled her and sworn to protect her forever. She knew that without a doubt and a part of her wanted it more than she wanted her next breath. But a bigger part of her wanted closure.

"He grabbed me, pushed me down on the bed and when I screamed for him to stop he just laughed. He called me Bunny, told me I'd always be his Bunny no matter where I went." Tears stung her eyes again but Monica in all her stubbornness dared them to fall. "It was the most pain I'd ever felt in my life and it wouldn't stop. Even when I couldn't yell anymore, when my arms couldn't swing any harder and my legs were frozen in place, it didn't stop. He didn't stop. The man that swore he loved me above all else for three years inflicted this awful pain on me. Then when he was finished he stood up and said if he ever found out I was with another man he'd kill me.

"For the next few days I stayed in that apartment wanting nothing more than to just die and be done with it. But then Deena called me to tell me about this modeling job she'd landed—modeling was her thing at the time. She sounded so excited and so full of life and at the end of the conversation she said, 'I love you, Monica.'"

The tears, damn them, fell as she said those last words and wondered why in all these years she'd forgotten that last part. She'd remembered everything about that night, every word out of Yates's mouth, but she hadn't remembered her baby sister telling her she loved her until this very moment.

"I figured if Deena loved me then I could live. I could get out of that apartment and go back home and live. And that's what I did."

"But you really didn't, did you, Monica? You were afraid to live because of his threat."

She nodded and swallowed. "I was afraid."

Alex did walk to her then. He reached out and wrapped his arms around her and held on tight. "I'm so sorry this happened to you. So sorry you had to endure all this at such a young age. It's not too late to prosecute him for the rape, you know."

She shook her head. "I know, but I have to think about that more." Reluctantly she pulled out of his grasp. "Just like I have to think about us more."

"About us? What's there to think about? I love you, Monica. I want to spend the rest of my life trying as hard as I can to deserve the strong, independent woman you've grown into."

"But I don't know if I want that from you, Alex. I don't know if I want your love and protection or if I even deserve it. I don't know this woman you claim to love because I feel like she's someone I pretended to be all these years. I need to know if I, if the real Monica Lakefield, loves you or even wants the type of commitment you're talking about."

"What are you saying?" Alex asked, his face hardening as he waited. "Just say it, Monica. Tell me no and mean it with your heart."

Monica took a deep breath and did what was possibly the hardest thing she'd had to do. "No, Alex. I don't want this with you right now. I'm saying no and meaning it with all my heart." The last words hitched as tears flowed freely once more. Her chest constricted, her heart hammering as if it would jump right out of her chest.

Alex nodded. He went to the closet, grabbed his bag and threw the clothes he'd had on yesterday inside then quietly walked out the door. Out of her life.

And Monica sat on the floor in the middle of her bedroom, wrapped only in a towel, and cried some more.

Chapter 23

Four weeks later

They'd been through so much in such a short span of time. Valentine's Day was almost over and here she was stepping off the elevator onto the twenty-third floor where the executive offices of Bennett Industries were located. Monica took a deep breath and walked with the confidence she was known for, the confidence that had been shaken a bit in the past couple of weeks, but was now back with a vengeance.

Alex told her once that when she said no with her heart he'd walk away. And he had. Monica thought her heart could never be broken as severely as it had been years ago by Yates. Now she knew an entirely different kind of hurt. Yates hurt her mentally and physically, he took a part of her she hadn't even learned to live with yet. He'd taken her youth, her idealism about love and relationships, and turned them into something ugly and dark. Then he'd threatened her life. Looking back it was probably more than foolish of her not to tell her family about what he'd done to her, or to tell someone so that at least she could move on with her life with some semblance of sanity.

Luckily and finally, she'd closed that chapter of her life. Yates was a part of her past and nothing more. She'd given him too much of herself as it was. And she hadn't given Alex enough. It was beyond humbling to realize that she'd wanted his love so much and had thrown it away under the pretense of protecting herself. Alex wanted to protect her and to love her and she'd been a fool. That's what Deena had said and Karena had agreed when they'd been on the three-way call days after she'd pushed Alex away. Although Karena hadn't been as vocal as Deena. It still amazed Monica that her baby sister had so much clarity and good sense when it came to relationships when all along Monica had found herself advising Deena.

"Who would have thought two of the Lakefield sisters would have to deal with a deranged stalker?" Deena had asked while they were on the phone, trying to lighten the mood that had been dampened by Monica's admission about the rape. "And in the end it was you that kicked both their asses!" Her baby sister had laughed at that.

"So now what are you going to do about Alex?" Karena had asked. "He really loves you, Monica."

"Yeah, and that's not an easy feat," Deena added.

"Okay, Deena, I get it."

"No, Monica, I don't think you do. You think everything has to happen in your time, according to your plan. But that's not how love works. It's not how life works. This man loves you, tried to protect you, wanted to give you the world and you pushed him away. Why? Because you were feeling sorry for yourself?"

"No, because I need to find myself."

"When exactly did you lose yourself? You've been the same strong-minded, ambitious, loyal sister every year of my life. You think Yates took something from you but he didn't—he unknowingly strengthened what was already there."

It had taken her a couple more days, then three weeks of therapy on Mondays and Wednesdays, to see how true Deena's words really were.

Now she was here, at the door to Alex's office. It was well after nine so the staff was all gone for the evening. Yet she'd known without a doubt this was where she'd find Alex. They were so alike in their business practices it was scary. She wondered briefly how a future with them would work considering their schedules, but brushed that thought off. No more negativity. No more protecting herself from the unknown. She was going for what she wanted, hoping against hope that he still wanted her.

After knocking on the door, she waited to hear his voice telling her to come in. When she didn't she almost turned to leave. But then the door opened and instead of hearing his voice she was blessed with seeing his handsome face.

"This is a surprise," he said.

His face was blank and Monica searched his eyes urgently, trying to pick up some emotion. If it was there, Alex hid it well.

"I probably should have called first, but honestly I knew you'd be here."

He nodded. "Do you want to come in?"

"Yes. Thanks."

He stepped to the side and she moved past him into his office. A very cordial act that did nothing to bolster her confidence. Behind her she heard him close and lock the door.

"So what brings you by? Is everything all right at the gallery?"

"The gallery is fine," she said, removing her leather jacket and placing it along with her purse on one of the guest chairs.

Alex had made his way around his desk and was just sitting in his chair. "Oh, Adriana thanks you implicitly for giving her Jaydon Donovan's number. She's going to Miami later this month to meet with her. And I think her older brother Dion is going to do some kind of article in their magazine about her transition."

Monica smiled sincerely. "I'm glad I could help. I really like your sisters, Alex. Your whole family is a great bunch of people. You're very lucky."

"Thank you."

She cleared her throat and sat up straight in the chair—old habits died hard.

"Why don't you just tell me what you're doing here, Monica?"

"You once called me Queen. I think you said I was your queen and that you wanted to spend the rest of your life loving me or something like that." She gave him a nervous smile, but he didn't return it.

"You also told me if I said no and meant it you would walk away. And you did."

"I did."

"That hurt me more than anything I thought ever could."

"That wasn't my intention. I was doing what you asked."

She nodded. "I know. But I have something else to ask you, Alex."

"Go ahead."

"I want you to be my king. You protected me when I was too stupid to accept it. You held me when I continuously tried to push you away. You loved a woman I didn't think deserved any man's love. You gave me back what I thought I'd lost. And for those reasons alone I am forever grateful to you."

"You came here to give me your gratitude?"

Another nervous laugh escaped and Monica decided this would work better if she stood.

"No. I came here to ask you, Alexander Bennett, to marry me."

When he opened his mouth to speak she held up a hand, stopping him.

"I'm not perfect, Alex. I'm stubborn and I can be selfish. I'm bossy and irritable and ambitious to a fault. I like things my way and I don't like to be told what to do. But I love you with all my heart and I'm hoping that'll be enough to bypass all the other bad points I just made."

He didn't say anything.

"You can talk now," she prodded.

But he still didn't say anything. Instead he stood from his chair and walked around the desk. When he was in front of her he leaned back, crossing his arms over his chest.

"It took a lot for you to come here, didn't it?" he asked.

"It did."

"What would you do if I said no and meant it with my heart?"

She'd go into a corner, curl up and die. No, she wouldn't, Monica thought with a slight pain in her chest. She'd survive just as she had before. "I'd be pretty damned pissed at you for a while and would curse you every time I saw you. But I would live, Alex. I would still live."

He smiled then. A big warm smile that had her nipples tingling and her heart filling.

"And what if I said yes? Would you come over here and kiss me or would you just stand there and smile?"

"I'd come over there and kiss you and kiss you until you couldn't breathe."

"That sounds good."

"Well?" she asked.

"Well what?"

"What's your answer?"

He crooked a finger, telling her to come closer. When she was standing right in front of him, close enough that she could smell his cologne and see the rise and fall of his chest as he breathed, Alex leaned forward and whispered in her ear.

"Yes."

Monica threw her arms around his neck and put her lips to his. She did exactly as she said she would; she kissed him and kissed him and kissed him some more.

* * * * *

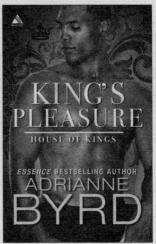

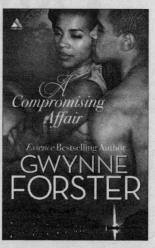

REQUEST YOUR FREE BOOKS!

2 FREE NOVELS
PLUS 2 FREE GIFTS!

KIMANI™
ROMANCE

Love's ultimate destination!

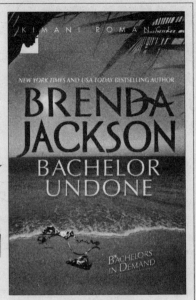